Abby—Into the Dragon's Den

BOOK 6 IN ABBY'S SOUTH SEAS ADVENTURES SERIES

DON'T MISS THE OTHER EXCITING TITLES!

SOUTH SEAS ADVENTURES

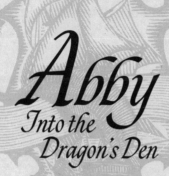

Abby
Into the Dragon's Den

PAMELA WALLS

TYNDALE HOUSE PUBLISHERS, INC.
WHEATON, ILLINOIS

Visit Tyndale's exciting Web site for kids at www.abbyadventures.com

Copyright © 2001 by Pamela Walls. All rights reserved.

Cover illustration copyright © 2001 by Jean Paul Tibbles/Bernstein and Andruilli. All rights reserved.

Interior map: Atlas Maluku. Landelijk Steunpunt Educatie Molukkers, Utrecht, The Netherlands 1998.

Scripture quotations are taken from the *Holy Bible,* New International Version®. NIV®. Copyright © 1973, 1978, 1984 by International Bible Society. Used by permission of Zondervan Publishing House. All rights reserved.

This novel is a work of fiction. Names, characters, places, and incidents are either the product of the author's imagination or are used fictitiously. Any resemblance to actual events, locales, organizations, or persons living or dead is entirely coincidental and beyond the intent of either the author or publisher.

ISBN 0-8423-3631-1

Printed in the United States of America

10 09 08 07 06 05 04 03 02 01
10   9   8   7   6   5   4   3   2   1

To Jean Paul Tibbles,
an artist whose heart is as big as his talent.
Thank you!

Writing is a solitary job, so I thank God for the
sweet encouragement He's brought me through
such kind friends—Kathy, Deirdre, Kim, Victoria,
Mary Anne, Pammy, Clarke, Bev, Mary Margaret,
Lilly, Maria, Kris, Claire, Jill, Hannah, Sarah,
Kay, Dana, Mackenzie, Robbie, Cathryn, and my
wonderful praying church family!

*My prayer is not that You take them out of the world
but that You protect them from the evil one.*
John 17:15

Chapter One

Abby Kendall's cinnamon curls whipped against her cheeks in the hot Indonesian wind. "Oh, bother!" she said, balancing her journal on her blue chambray skirt and pushing her hair out of her eyes. To port they were passing a green island with mangroves along a sometimes rocky coast. Abby dug into her skirt pocket for a bit of ribbon to tie back her hair which, she was sure, had a rebellious mind of its own.

"I don't see that island on our map," she heard Luke Quiggley say as he leaned over the chart table next to Duncan MacIndou, their ship's captain. An orphan and Abby's best friend, Luke had traveled with her family from California to Hawaii. Now that the Kendalls had begun their own shipping business with Duncan, Luke's aunt, Dagmar Gronen, had given him permission to sail the South Seas with them. "According to this morning's sightings," 14-year-old Luke continued, "we should be about here. But the island we're passing isn't charted."

1

Duncan adjusted his black eye patch and peered at the map. "Yer right, Luke. It's not there. But this is an old chart I found when I bought the ship in San Francisco. And there are thousands of islands in the rrregion—many probably aren't mapped yet."

After months of traveling with Duncan, Abby still enjoyed the captain's Scottish brogue. She closed her journal and joined them at the chart table. Pointing to some fancy lettering on the yellowed paper, Abby asked, "Why does the map have that strange saying on it—*Here Be Dragons*?"

Luke, who loved adventure as much as Abby, snorted at her comment. "Dragons? Ha! Everyone knows there's no such things."

Duncan twirled his dark handlebar moustache. One eyebrow arched as he said, "I wouldna be too sure of that, laddie. In me own wee town in Scotland there are tales of old, tales that make yer blood run cold. Have ye not heard of mythical beasts that eat humans—to say nothing of sheep and puppies?" He glanced at Abby and winked playfully.

Abby's deep blue eyes sparkled. She could feel a story coming. Nine-year-old Sarah, who had been at the helm with Ma, must have overheard Duncan for she quickly joined Abby and Luke, towing Luke's yellow puppy, Sandy, behind her. Gazing up at the Scotsman, she said, "Tell us about the monsters, Duncan!"

"I thought ye'd never ask," Duncan said, motioning for them to sit on the bulkhead as he pulled out a pocketknife and began whittling a piece of sandal-wood. Abby glanced over at Ma, whose mink-brown hair stayed in an amazingly perfect braid as she steered the *Kamana*. She smiled when the Scottish investigator-turned-captain began his tale.

"A long time ago," Duncan said in hushed tones, "before all the unicorns and fairies disappeared, there was known in the northern regions of my homeland a terrible fierce dragon named Snord the Ferocious. This beast had three horns sprrrouting from his forehead—as sharp as swords. And the blast of his breath could incinerate half a village in a giant flame."

Sarah's eyes were round as steel-blue marbles. She stared at the one-eyed captain as he continued.

"Fer many centuries the dragon exacted a price from all the villages in the region. Each month a different hamlet provided sheep for his dinner, mutton being the favorite dish of dragons, as ye know. Ten sheep were demanded. The poor things were staked on a hill near the village. Then, in the dark of night, the dragon would fly in from his lair in the craggy mountains. The villagers always knew when the sheep had been eaten because when the dragon burped, fire erupted from him in a giant belch. They could see the flame from a great distance away."

Sarah frowned. "It's not nice to eat sheep," she objected. "Think how their mothers must have felt."

"Aye," Duncan agreed. "'Twasn't nice at all. But then, some dragons haven't got a kind bone in their bodies."

Abby glanced at Luke, who sat cross-legged next to her in his rolled-up duckcloth sailor pants. He smiled at Duncan's comment while he practiced tying knots on a line.

"Before long, 'twas the turn of the poorest village in the region to give up their yearly offering of 10 sheep. Unfortunately, this village had seen hard times that year. There were only eight sheep left in all the village, and one of those was the pet of a fatherless boy named Stuart.

"Poor Stuart had problems of his own: his father had died the year before. He'd been a sailor and had returned from a voyage with a barrel of Chinese rice and another of Indian spice called *curry* as a gift to his wife. But, alas, he died while sailing in a storm the following winter, so Stuart became the man of the house at the tender age of 11."

Duncan leaned close to Abby and Sarah as he spoke. "Truth was, Stuart was the smallest boy in the shire for his age—and he was often teased about it. On top of that," Duncan said, "he had the reddest hair ye've ever seen—'twas the color of a shiny copper penny."

Abby frowned sympathetically. She'd heard her share of "carrottop" comments.

"Since he was teased unmercifully by all the bigger boys of the village, Stuart's best friend became his sheep. He called her "Curly" and loved her fiercely. But the town leaders said he must sacrifice her to the dragon, to keep the poor village safe."

Sarah bit her lower lip anxiously. "Oh no! Not his pet." She bent down and patted Sandy, who was getting too big to carry now. "Up, girl," she ordered, and Sandy gladly jumped up and settled in Sarah's lap, her white-tipped tail wagging contentedly.

"Aye, 'twas a dark day for Stuart. Made all the worse because his mother was sick in bed, and much of their income depended on Curly's fine wool. From this, his mother made sweaters. But in only a week's time, he would have to give Curly up to the village leaders.

"That night, Stuart went to bed with tears on his cheeks and a prayer on his lips. 'Heavenly Father,' he prayed, 'help me find a way to save Curly!' And as he slept, a dream came to him. So in the morning light he knew what he must do—aye, but thinking of it made his stomach clench into a knot," Duncan said, balling his fist into a knot to make his point.

"What did he do?" Sarah urged.

"Well, back then it was common knowledge that dragons have a sweet tooth," Duncan explained. "And Snord the Ferocious was no different. Of course, their favorite food is mutton and maidens, but shortbread is a close second. So Stuart began to assemble the ingredients for sweet cake: eggs, flour, and last summer's honey. But it wasn't long before he ran out and had to go through the whole village, trading work for the necessary supplies. Late at night when he returned home from his chores, he stoked the fire and baked. By week's end he had 28 special cakes. So that when the village leaders came to take Curly, Stuart was not without hope.

"He set the cakes in a small wooden wagon and pulled it down the same path that the village fathers had taken Curly and the other sheep. He watched from a distance as they staked the poor frightened sheep to the hillside, which was charred from last year's dragon feast."

Now Abby and Luke were listening attentively. Abby reached over and petted Sandy absently. The ship heeled in a sudden gust of wind, making Abby look up to see that they were passing an island village set along the coast. Bamboo homes on stilts squatted near the water's edge. In the distance she could see dark-haired islanders. Abby bent back to her opened journal and started drawing.

Duncan's voice dropped an octave. "Night fell. The wind whipped up, cold and raw, for spring was still a month away. The sheep bleated, as if asking for help, when Stuart arrived among them. 'Don't be afraid,' he told them. He uncorked the small barrel of Indian spice and began to powder the animals' fleece with it. Its scent was strong and biting, and he hoped it would keep the dragon from gobbling them up before his plan took effect.

"As the black night deepened, a rush of wings was

heard upon the wind. Stuart gazed at the moon—all ghostly pale and shrouded in clouds. Then the largest creature he'd ever seen flew out of the mists and came circling down on silver wings. Stuart's poor wee heart almost stopped in fear. But he remembered the dream and stood tall—er, as tall as possible for the shortest boy of the village."

Sarah wrung her hands. Abby glanced at Luke, but he was lifting his eyes to see what shadow had crossed the deck. A cloud had covered the sun momentarily.

"When the dragon swooped down and landed near the sheep, they erupted in terrified bleating, trying to break free. Stuart wanted to calm them, but his throat was almost too dry to speak. Then the dragon pounded toward the sheep and stretched out its gigantic claws.

" 'Wait!' Stuart shouted. 'I have a special treat made just to honor you, O Snord the Magnificent.' Well, everyone knows dragons are extremely prideful and can't resist a compliment. The scaled lizard turned toward the voice and licked his lips.

" 'Who is addressing me?' His voice was like thunder and Stuart could feel his knees trembling.

" 'Yer humble servant,' Stuart managed to squeak out with a bow.

"The dragon laughed and sat down. 'I find,' Snord said, 'that compliments improve the flavor of mutton. Speak up, boy!'

" 'Why, yer lordship, ye are the most magnificent dragon I've ever seen,' Stuart said.

" 'That is obvious,' the dragon said. 'What else?'

" 'Ah . . . yer power is unequaled among those who walk the earth. Yer scales are the shiniest, yer breath the deadliest, yer horns the sharpest in all the land!'

"Snord lay back, his belly covered with 1,000 scales. Stuart could see there was no way through that tough hide, even if he'd had a sword.

" 'Oh, magnificent and powerful Snord, if it please ye, would ye care to try one of the cakes I've prepared to honor ye?' With that Stuart dramatically wrenched the cloth off the cakes and stood back. The dragon's nostrils widened instantly. He sat up and sniffed.

" 'Aye, they are for the ferocious Snord, who is legendary in these parts,' Stuart said. 'It is only yer due.'

"Snord frowned. 'Speaking of my due, I count only eight sheep. And they smell awful! Do the villagers think to cheat me from the 10 they owe me? Do they think that a stick of a boy can equal two plump sheep? You're not more than a tasty morsel,' he said, and his eyes began to glow with the fire of hunger.

" 'Try a cake!' Stuart blurted out with a clumsy bow. The giant's claws, as long as an ax, came toward him and snatched up a cake and tossed it into his mouth. A look of ecstasy came over him and his eyes closed a moment.

" 'How about another, O splendid one?'

"Before long, the dragon had consumed all 28 cakes. 'I will lie down for a spell before I eat those worthless, stinking sheep,' Snord said. 'And you.'

"While the dragon lay snoring on his back, Stuart watched his belly rise and fall with each dragon breath. Gradually, the boy began to smile. You see, Snord's belly was growing larger and larger with every snore, and only Stuart knew why. He had hidden in each cake several hollowed-out eggshells filled with uncooked rice. As each cake was swallowed by the great beast, his raspy gullet broke the eggshells and sent the uncooked rice into his belly."

Abby grinned with dawning understanding as Duncan rubbed his palms together gleefully. "As ye well know, a dragon's belly is full of fire. And that rice began to swell and cook. It puffed up and up and up until the beast was as roly-poly as ol' King Cole."

Sarah looked relieved. "Did Curly get away?"

"Aye. When the dragon awoke, he couldn't eat another bite. 'Besides, those sheep stink!' he told Stuart. 'Take them away. I am full enough until next month.' And with that he belched a gigantic burp, almost turning the sheep to roasted mutton in the process. Stuart didn't wait for Snord to change his mind but led the sheep toward home."

"What'd his ma think when he brought back Curly?" Luke asked. Abby's heart went out to him, for she knew he was thinking of his own dear ma, whom he wouldn't see again until he reached heaven.

Duncan gave Luke a knowing look. "His ma was proud, but then she always believed in him. The villagers, however, had seen the dragon's flame from a distance and thought all the sheep were gone. But the next morn, when they saw wee Stuart leading their sheep into town and heard about his daring adventure, they declared he'd grown a foot overnight! No one ever teased Stuart about his height again. Of course," Duncan added with a wink, "he did grow up to be a tall, handsome man."

Abby looked hopeful. "So his copper hair turned a lovely mahogany shade as he got older?"

"Nay," Duncan replied with a shake of his head. "But he married a bonnie girl who liked it bright as a copper penny. She said it would always remind them of the dragon's flame and her husband's bravery."

Luke grinned. "See, Carrottop," he teased, "you might turn out all right after all."

"Luke Quiggley," Abby said with a growl as she jumped up and ran after him across the sloping deck, "you're a varmint with dragon breath!"

He ducked under the boom, laughing, and started climbing up the ratlines to escape her. Sarah jumped up and down, her red dress billowing and her white-blonde hair falling out of its braids. "Get him, Abby," she encouraged her sister. "Even if what he says about your hair *is* true!"

Abby climbed the ratlines after Luke, though she felt unsteady as the ship dipped into swells. Luke was already high above her, and she didn't relish going much higher. She hated heights.

"Hey!" Luke cried out. "Land ho!"

She stared at him with a frown. "We've been passing that island for the past 20 minutes, you silly goose."

"What I mean is, mansion ho!" Luke pointed toward a pale blue bay with white sand ringing it. Above the water, on a gentle slope dotted with coconut palms, stood a lovely English mansion. Greenery surrounded it on three sides.

"Oh, my . . ." Abby hung on the ratlines, taking in the scene. "I smell a new scent," she said to Uncle Samuel, who'd just arrived from below the deck. "It's a sweeter fragrance than the ocean brine."

Her biologist uncle paused to rub his pork-chop sideburns. "I smell it, too, almost like . . ."

"Pumpkin pies!" Sarah said enthusiastically.

"Nutmeg!" Ma offered from the helm as she steered the ship. Pa got up from his spot at the bow where he'd been repairing a sail.

Duncan came to the port railing. "It's not a true Spice Island—those are northeast of here," he said. "But it could well be a spice plantation."

Abby climbed down and stood on the deck. "Oh, let's go see who lives there." She was tired of being on board ship. They had just sailed from China— where they'd traded sugar for silk—when Uncle

Samuel had convinced them to head to the Banda Sea to explore Indonesia before returning home to Hawaii. Pa and Duncan hoped to pick up some valuable spices for trade as well. But it'd been a long sail, even if she did love every one of the eight people on board—all of them family except Luke, Duncan, and Duncan's beautiful half sister, Lani.

Like a nimble monkey, Luke now climbed down the ratlines to join Abby on deck. His green eyes danced with determination as he pointed toward shore. "There's a freshwater creek running down to the sea over there," he added. She knew he was reminding the grown-ups that they needed to make a watering stop.

Pa came toward them, rubbing his neck where his dark blond hair curled over his collar. "Truth is," he said to Duncan, "we *are* running low on fresh water. That hot southerly wind has dried us all out."

"And," Ma said, "this island carries an inviting fragrance."

Duncan nodded. "Yer rrright. Let's anchor for a few nights. We can stock up on water, fresh fruit, maybe even some fresh game. And Abby," he said, turning to her, "can satisfy that curious mind of hers."

Luke chuckled. "She gets it honest. Uncle Samuel can hardly wait to see new Indonesian critters."

Even as Luke uttered his last word, Uncle Samuel was hurrying below to gather his day pack, journal, and pencils. "Lani," the biologist called out to Duncan's half-Hawaiian sister, "we're going ashore! Get your most comfortable walking shoes for a jungle hike!" Abby grinned at the warmth in her uncle's voice. Since China, sparks had been flying between beautiful Lani and Uncle Samuel. *If this keeps up,* Abby thought, *those sparks of love are bound to burst into flame.*

Abby leaned toward Luke. "Who knows," she whispered, "maybe we'll discover dragons and magical beasts here." She opened her journal, which was filled with drawings and poems, and pointed to a pencil sketch she'd done of a knight in shining armor fighting a mythical flying lizard. The knight was trying valiantly to rescue a fair maiden from the dragon's claws.

Luke glanced casually at the drawing. "It's lucky that dragons have disappeared," he quipped, "because I left my armor at home, Miss Abigail of the Round Table."

Abby ignored his comment. "Just think, we're going to investigate an uncharted island. It's a mystery just waiting to be discovered! Maybe we'll find new creatures or make a new friend. . . ."

Even as Ma steered the *Kamana* into the bay, Abby could hear faint sounds of bird cries coming from the dense green jungle. Luke jumped to help Pa and Uncle Samuel take in the mainsail, while Duncan let down the anchor.

Abby knew she should be helping, but she

couldn't stop staring at the mountain that dominated the island. Its cone shape loomed—dark and forbidding—over the tiny tropical kingdom. She couldn't see the top. It was wreathed in clouds and swirling mists and, for just a moment, Abby imagined it would be the perfect place for dragons to live.

Chapter Two

Abby gripped the gunwales of the rowboat as Duncan and Luke rowed them all to shore. Sarah held Sandy in her lap as the boat rode the swells. The water was so clear that Abby could see white coral heads and yellow and blue fish darting among the castlelike growths. The waves were gentle, and the boat washed safely up on the beach.

Ma had stored their lunch in Uncle Samuel's day pack, and they all looked forward to a picnic under the coconut palms. But first they needed to greet the mansion dwellers and ask permission to use their beach. Although Abby could hardly wait to meet some new friends, she fell behind the others. She'd inherited Ma's weak legs and found walking in the sand a slow, hard process.

Ma, who'd had a head start, paused to wait for her and put an arm around Abby's waist as they reached the rise. "Since we're going to be here a few days," Ma said, "why don't we take a break from book learning?"

Abby almost shouted for joy until Charlotte

Kendall went on. "Go study the island life with Uncle Samuel, take some field hikes with him, then turn in a report on how this island differs from the Hawaiian Islands."

Abby's face screwed up in a pucker. Even though she loved learning, she'd hoped for a little vacation from it.

"Come on, slowpokes!" Sarah stamped her foot on the sandy path ahead, her white-blonde hair shining in the sunlight. "Let's hurry up and meet these people so we can have our picnic."

"Shhh," Ma scolded.

"She does have a point," Luke whispered to Abby as she caught up to him.

When Luke's stomach grumbled, she shot him a whimsical look. "You're always hungry, Luke."

"I'm just growing, Abby. It's hard to stop that process." She glanced up at his tanned face and blond-streaked hair. Almost 15, Luke was as tall as many men and the work on board ship had filled him out, not to mention Ma's good cooking. But it did seem like he'd sprouted up another inch— almost as fast as Stuart in the tale Duncan had told, Abby thought.

As they approached the overgrown walk leading to the mansion's double front doors, they heard Pa shout in a friendly voice, "Hello, anyone home?" Duncan was knocking on the door with the rusted brass door knocker, although one of the doors already stood ajar.

Abby's eyes skimmed the white mansion quickly. Faded green shutters hung askew on loose hinges at the windows, which were wide open. Tattered curtains billowed out from them in the breeze. Vines, growing up the front of the mansion, appeared to be crawling right into the house through the windows. But although the mansion was run-down, Abby could see that once it had been elegant.

"Perhaps no one lives here," Lani said. When she turned to smile shyly at Uncle Samuel, her silky chestnut hair swung below her waist in the hot breeze.

"It does look deserted," Abby agreed.

Sarah's slate-blue eyes, which rarely missed a detail, were full of concern. "Don't go in, Pa. It looks haunted. Maybe monsters live here."

"Sarah, wherever did you get such an idea?" Ma asked.

"There's no such things as monsters and dragons, short stuff," Luke said, patting her on the head.

But when a sudden piercing scream erupted inside the mansion, Abby thought Sarah just might be right.

"Someone needs help!" Pa shouted as he sprinted the last few steps and pushed into the house behind Duncan.

Within seconds, the entire family was crowded on the threshold, peering in to see if someone had been mortally hurt. When the screech came again,

Duncan, who was in the lead, laughed and ducked. "'Tis only a parrot," he said, pointing to the flash of green-and-yellow wings that landed on torn curtains at the window.

The bird cocked its head at them. "Shiver me timbersss . . . I'm Nutmeg!"

Sarah's mouth dropped open. "That bird is talking to us."

Before anyone could respond, another scream jolted them. This time a tiny black ape, no bigger than the monkeys Abby had seen in books, flew off a crystal chandelier and landed on a long wooden bench in the front parlor. The chandelier still swung wildly as the creature jumped up and down on the worn-out bench pillows, chattering at them with teeth bared. Sarah gripped Ma's hand and leaned against her.

Abby thought about doing the same thing when a snorting sound came from their left, down a hallway. She inched closer to Luke as they waited to see what would emerge from the hall.

"A pig!" Sarah shouted as a black piglet snorted and snuffled its way past them, waddling under a set of swinging doors that led to what Abby guessed might be the cooking area in the back of the house.

Sandy barked protectively at the collection of noisy creatures, and Luke bent down and hushed her.

"Why, I never," Ma whispered in amazement.

"It's an animal mansion, Ma," Sarah said joyfully, letting go of her hand. "Wild critters live here!"

The family stared in amazement at the run-down interior of the mansion while the tailless black ape jumped up and down and scolded them like a little old man. The parrot made another pass overhead, and a small beige-and-brown goat wandered in through the front door, still chewing flowers from the front yard.

At that instant, a tiny Indonesian woman emerged through the swinging doors, wiping her hands on a dish towel. Her gray hair was pinned up in a bun, and she wore a wraparound straight skirt of brown with a gold cotton blouse tucked in. "What is all this noise—," she began, obviously speaking to the ape, when she glanced up and spotted Abby's clan. "Oh, my!"

Pa cleared his throat. "We didn't mean to frighten you, ma'am. We knocked, but no one heard us. And we thought the place was deserted." Pa looked around the busy room with a grin. "But we were wrong!"

The woman stood still for a moment, her tiny frame bent with age, then she smiled. Her face instantly flooded with a kind light. "You are welcome here," she said, nodding her head in a bow. Her accented voice rose and dipped like a melody. "I have had few visitors for many years, and I am happy to have guests!"

Abby could see real joy in her eyes as she continued. "I am Sulia. I have lived here most of my life." She called to the young ape. Instantly it bounded over and leapt into her arms. "These animals, they keep me company. Paloa, my granddaughter, brings me all the injured creatures she finds in the jungle, and I don't have the heart to throw them out."

Pa quickly introduced each of the ship's crew to Sulia and explained that they had come to re-water the ship and pick fruit, with her permission.

Sulia seemed pleased. "You must stay and refresh from your travel. I have many bedrooms. Mrs. Cleets, the original owner of this mansion, left most of the furniture, so you each may have a bed. I will be most happy for your company."

Ma, who seemed to like Sulia already, asked her to join them in their lunch meal on the beach. "No, no. You stay here to eat," Sulia insisted. So they all sat at the long dining-room table, after brushing bird feathers off it, and laid out their supply of bread, coconut, and dried fish.

Sulia hurried to the kitchen and came back with several of the island's bananas. Sarah's eyes bugged out. "Those bananas are big enough for Paul Bunyan!" she said.

"Why, they're over two feet long," Luke said.

Sulia nodded and handed one to Pa. He sliced it up as she hurried back to the kitchen again. Inside were large black seeds that surprised them all. Ma followed to help. She and Sulia returned carrying cups and a tall pitcher of red liquid. "It is hibiscus

make your aquaintaince." She looked to her grandmother, who nodded encouragement.

"She has not spoken English to anyone but me,"
Sulia explained. "Her father forbids it in the
village."

"You speak good," Sarah piped up, as she rose to
pet the young goat on its head. "Is this your pet?"

"Yes," Paloa answered. "He is special. Few goats
are pure brown as Timor—most have white-and-
gray markings on them." She set the kid down, but
he bleated unhappily. Paloa reached down to pet
him. "He thinks I'm his mother," she said with a
giggle.

Sandy the pup bounded out from under the table
toward the goat, sniffing at his cloven hooves.
"Woof!" Sandy barked. But a moment later Timor
put his nose to Sandy's, and the puppy's tail began
to wag.

"Look, they're friends!" Sarah said. "How old are
you, Paloa?"

"Eleven years. And you?" she asked.

Soon the children were sharing information like
they were old friends. Paloa was thrilled to meet
other young Christians for the first time.

"Come—," Paloa urged, "I will show you my
secret grotto. I don't bring my other friends there
because they can't come to the mansion with me.
But you won't be here long and—" she paused, then
said shyly—"I don't have any other friends who are

Christians like Grandmother and me. It is special to know you."

Abby smiled at Paloa's friendly face. "I'd love to see it."

"Me, too," Sarah offered.

"Me, three," Luke chuckled as they headed out the back kitchen door.

Behind the mansion was a wide lake with tall nutmeg trees beyond it. The tropical forest encroached on each side of the lake, and the mountain loomed not too far in the distance. The sweet scent of dried clove flowers and the cries of birds filled the air, telling Abby she was in a strange new world.

Abby, Luke, and Sarah followed close behind as Paloa led them to the right of the mansion and under the forest canopy, where the light turned a pale green. Huge ferns grew, just like in Hawaii, Abby thought. But in the moist tropical heat there were far more orchids here and other flowers that seemed to grow right out of the air itself. They covered tree trunks and hung from branches as if some skilled gardener had planned it just to delight them.

The whir of many insect wings and the high-pitched cries of birds and geckos were constant. Up above them, the treetops swayed in the wind. But on the ground it was hot and moist, with sweet scents of ginger, frangipani, and wet earth. Long vines flowed down from branches like thin green waterfalls. Luke reached out and ran a hand down one smooth vine. "Look," he said, "they pile up on the ground like green snake coils."

Paloa smiled. "Be careful. There are green snakes here, too."

"And look at the tiny monkeys up in the trees!" Abby said, laughing.

"Those are tarsiers," Paloa explained.

No bigger than Luke's hand, they chattered and leapt from limb to limb. But even as they watched and walked, the noises above suddenly took on a different quality. The chattering turned into screeches and screams, and the small mammals seemed to fly through the air. Dark crows swooped from their resting spots, cawing loudly, and lifted away.

"Something's after them," Paloa said. "A predator."

They scanned the tree limbs as the mammals overhead jumped as fast as greased lightning.

Soon most of the tarsiers had moved so far ahead that Abby could no longer see them, but one little tarsier seemed lost. The others had leapt a great distance from one branch to another, but now the young creature paused in fright. Apparently it wasn't sure it could bridge the great distance to the next tree. Abby watched it look over its shoulder, and her heart clutched at its plight. With her weak legs, she was always the last, too!

Suddenly behind it streaked a blur of dark snake

scales. The little monkey flew off its perch, sailed through the air, and just barely landed on a swaying branch. In hot pursuit, the predator went after it but missed the branch. It landed with a loud *whomp* on the mossy forest floor. For a moment, it lay still.

Sarah screamed, jumping back in fright.

Chapter Three

"That's got to be the biggest lizard in the world!" Luke said, stepping back as well. It stood almost two feet high as it stretched its neck up. It was easily three feet long but seemed bigger because of its thickset muscular body. As they watched, the reptile turned toward them. A bright yellow tongue snaked out of its hissing mouth.

"Stay back!" Paloa warned, panic in her voice. Abby's palms began to sweat at the fear she saw in Paloa.

"That is an *ora*." Paloa swallowed hard. "Its bite is deadly!"

"It's ugly as sin," Luke said. "With that flat head, it looks like a thick snake on legs."

"Only meaner," Abby whispered, her eyes widening as the lizard began to move. "Watch out!" she yelled. "It's coming toward us!"

The creature took several rapid steps toward them, pounding the ground. Its long tongue swept the air for their scent, like a snake that could taste fear molecules.

Luke bent down and picked up a stout stick as the creature hissed and came on. But suddenly it stopped, as if it sensed something, then scurried off into the underbrush.

Abby heard Paloa sigh. "That was close. And very odd to see since they usually stay in the treetops. But come on, we're almost at my secret spot, where there's lots of sunshine and no trees overhead."

Sarah took Paloa's hand. "No *oras* allowed?" she questioned.

"Never!" Paloa said as she led the way. "Only treats from Grandmother and treasures from shipwrecks."

Soon Paloa led them out of the tropical forest into an open glade where a rainbow of flowers carpeted the ground. The ground swelled slightly, and Abby could see no secret grotto anywhere. As they climbed to the top of the small rise, Paloa said, "Down this way."

Now Abby understood. The rise had hidden a deep chasm in the ground. They stood on the edge and gazed over the rim into a secret cavern.

Abby gulped as she saw the narrow path that snaked down to the cavern floor about 20 feet below. She *really* hated heights. But when Sarah grabbed Paloa's hand and started down the winding path, Abby followed, her high boots sliding on loose pebbles.

Luke whistled as he traipsed behind her. "Look! A hot spring."

Abby followed Luke's pointing finger and saw a small steaming pool ringed with black rocks at one end of the wide cavern. Mist sprayed from it continuously, watering the flowers and ferns growing on the nearby cavern walls. Boulders littered the cavern floor. Near the other end a young frangipani tree blossomed, its scent sweet and pleasant. Abby knew that this same tree was called *plumeria* by the Hawaiians. Patches of ferns sprouted all over, and Abby noticed a few unlit torches in the ground.

"This *is* a secret grotto, Paloa. How enchanting!" Abby instantly longed for her journal. She had to capture this place on paper.

"No one else comes here?" Luke asked as he helped Abby down the crumbling trail.

"My father is the headman of the village," Paloa said as she continued helping Sarah. "In the last two years, he has forbidden my people to come near the mansion. He is angry at Grandmother, and I do not know why." She stopped suddenly on the path and gazed off in the distance. Abby watched her chew her lower lip before continuing. "Grandmother won't live in the village because our God is not welcome there. When my mother died, right after I was born, Father turned back to the old gods. He led all of our people back to the old ways. He was never a Christian, but Grandmother said he used to listen to her read the Bible until the day my mother died. Then he said if he'd given sacrifices to the old gods, she might have lived."

"But," Luke said, "your father lets you visit your grandma."

"Yes, because it is our way—it is *adat*—good manners to make sure your parents are taken care of in their old age. He would not be respected if he did not honor her, so I bring food and comfort to her." Paloa paused. "But I know Grandmother misses my father, Kaliman, very much."

As they continued to the bottom of the cavern in silence, Abby felt sorry for her new friend. Paloa was caught between the two people she loved most, and there seemed to be no way to solve her predicament. *If only there was some way to make things right, bring them together again for Paloa's sake,* she thought.

As soon as they reached the bottom of the chasm, Abby could see that Paloa had turned the area into her own charming palace. Paloa led them to a shallow cave on one side of the larger cavern. Inside, veils and silk pieces hung from rock walls, wooden slats from crates had been turned into tables and shelves, and broken crockery held baby ferns and flowers.

Sarah gushed, "What a grand place to play house."

Luke grimaced at that idea. "Where did you get all this stuff?"

Paloa gave a secretive smile. "A shipwreck. I have a secret passage to the beach." She motioned for them to follow as she led them to the right. A dark shadow loomed in the wall, and as they neared it Abby saw that it was an opening.

"This leads to the ocean," Paloa explained proudly. "It is a short walk—maybe 15 minutes through this cave."

"I don't like going in the dark too much," Sarah said, "and this tunnel gives me a creepy feeling."

"Let's go through it," Luke said eagerly. "I'd like to see where it comes out." He was already standing a few feet inside it. "Hey, I think I can hear waves. Listen!"

Abby joined him and stood with her head cocked. "It sounds like a seashell does when you put it to your ear and you can hear the ocean."

Curious, Sarah entered in a few feet. "You're right! But it's still too dark in here."

Paloa smiled at her. "It's all right, Sarah. I have torches we can take with us. I never go in caves without a firebrand."

They followed Paloa back to her little cave and watched her dig through objects on an old sea trunk. Resting on the trunk were lots of things: string, some paints and two brushes, an old weathered book, and something that was flat, about 12 inches high, and covered in old sailcloth.

"What's under that wrap?" Abby asked.

"A picture," Paloa answered, but she didn't offer to show it to them. Perhaps it was something Paloa had painted, and she was shy about showing it.

"Here they are," Paloa said, holding up a small wooden box of precious matches. "Let's go."

As they left the shallow cave, Luke pointed in the

opposite direction toward a dark shadow in the cavern wall. "What's that?"

"Another tunnel—but I've never gone in too far."

"Why not?" Abby asked.

"It leads toward the volcano, Mount Bakat. Sometimes I can hear it rumbling angrily through that cave, and it scares me. Besides, I once saw scorpions in there. So I won't go in alone—if I got hurt, there's no one here to help me."

Luke immediately looked interested, but Abby stopped him short. "Not now, Luke." She wasn't eager to go into a cave that grumbled!

As soon as Paloa's torch flared brightly, Luke offered to carry it. The two of them guided the way into the tunnel that led toward the ocean.

"Abby," Sarah whispered, "will you hold my hand?"

"Sure," Abby said as they headed into the closed-in space. The torchlight danced over the stone walls, showing off the rocky floor enough so Abby didn't trip. Luke was hooting now and then, and his voice echoed around them. The longer they hiked, the more Abby noticed moisture on the walls of the cave. When Luke quit talking, Abby could hear the sound of waves getting louder.

"We must be near the exit," she said, "I can hear—"

A roaring filled the glistening cave. Abby thought a freight train might be thundering toward them, for small rocks were dislodged from overhead. The ground trembled and loose dirt from the walls crumbled and fell. Sarah gripped Abby's hand painfully when they pitched forward. As Sarah hit Luke's knees, he dropped the torch and it sputtered in the water at their feet. Just as the light went out, the ground quit shaking, but in the pitch-black Sarah's terrified scream ricocheted off the walls.

The last thing Abby saw was Luke grabbing for the torch. When he picked it up, one side of it flared back to life. In the dim light, Abby saw the look on Paloa's face—a look of fear that told her this was not something she normally experienced.

"Let's go!" Luke urged, as he turned to check on Abby and Sarah. "You okay, short stuff?"

Sarah sniffed and nodded. They followed Luke quickly, stepping over stones that had tumbled loose and hurrying on. Now the rock walls seemed to close in on Abby. No one spoke until they saw a light at the end of the underground tunnel. Waves crashing onshore had never sounded so welcome before, Abby thought.

Sarah sped ahead of her, and soon Abby was the last one in the cave. She could see the others outlined against the sunlight 20 feet ahead. She smelled the ocean's briny scent. Abby watched her feet so she wouldn't trip as she hurried forward, then came to a crashing halt when she almost stepped on something bright and slithering.

Crossing the rock floor was a five-foot-long

snake. Abby moved her foot just in time but ended up straddling the serpent. Her skirt almost brushed it as she regained her balance and stepped backward.

A scream tore out of her.

Chapter Four

The snake had beautiful bright bands of red, yellow, green, white, and black.

Luke and Paloa ran toward her. "Stop!" she yelled, pointing to the banded snake.

Luke put a hand out to stop Paloa.

"Is it poisonous?" Abby asked from a safe distance now.

"Yes, it's *ular tjintamani,* the jeweled viper," Paloa said. "But if you aren't bitten, my people believe it brings good luck."

"That means if I survive meeting it," Abby muttered, "I'm supposed to have a good week?"

That made Paloa giggle, but Abby kept her eye on the viper. The snake kept moving off the path and toward a rock outcropping near the entrance. In another minute it disappeared under a large rock at the cave opening, and Abby hurried by and joined them in the sunlight.

She brushed back her curls and tucked her

blouse, which had come loose, into her skirt waist-band. Glancing up, she saw the Banda Sea breaking in the distance. They had emerged on a sloping cliffside above the ocean and perhaps 50 yards from the breakers. Salt spray and sea wind cooled them immediately.

"There's no way to get to the top of the cliff," Luke said, staring upward, "at least not any safe way."

"No," Paloa said, "I always head down. It's not too hard." After navigating the rocky cliff they were on, they'd have to walk down a sandy incline toward the distant palms and mangrove trees near the water.

Relieved to be out in the open, Abby gazed up the long curving shore. "Look, our ship is just a mile or two away." Resting on the curved beach was their ship's dinghy.

"Yes," agreed Paloa, who suddenly pointed, "and there is a nest we can reach on the way down!"

Abby was confused. "Why do we want to reach that bird's nest?"

"For a treat, of course," Paloa said, as if it were the most obvious thing in the world. Ahead of Abby, she was already reaching to loosen the nest from its spot between two stones.

Luke, who looked as confused as Abby felt, offered to carry it for Paloa. Sarah stayed near Luke as she descended without any problem.

"Do the islanders here consider bird eggs a

special treat?" Abby asked when she reached the others. She glanced at the odd nest with two brown eggs in it. Feathers littered the bottom of it. "The nest looks sort of . . ." Abby couldn't figure out why it looked different from other nests.

"It feels stiff," Luke offered.

"Yes!" Abby said. He'd hit it squarely.

"Of course," Paloa said patiently as they walked along, "that is because the mother bird uses her spit to glue the nest together. That is what makes bird's nest soup so delicious."

Luke quickly handed the nest back to Paloa.

Sarah stopped walking and squinted at Paloa. "Are you telling us that you make soup out of this nest that's full of bird spit?"

"It's delicious—a rare treat on my island." Paloa smiled contentedly.

Luke caught Abby's wide-eyed expression and shook his head no. But Abby couldn't help grinning. She'd never known him to turn down any food but the fermented Hawaiian staple called *poi*.

"I'm sure this is just as good as *poi*," she teased, "your favorite *purple* thing to eat."

He gave her a shrewd look. "I've hogged too many favorite treats, Abigail. I think this time I should leave it all to you and Sarah."

"Not me!" Sarah assured him quietly. "I'd rather boil up Sandy's sleeping blanket and eat that for dinner."

As the kids tromped in the back door of the mansion through the kitchen, they could hear Ma and Sulia laughing in the front room. Opened on Sulia's lap was her Bible, and the two of them were having a wonderful discussion.

"Look, Grandmother," Paloa said, rushing into the parlor. "We found a perfect bird's nest for dinner, and we saw a jeweled snake!"

"An exciting day," Sulia said, her eyes beaming with delight. "Did you feel the earthquake?"

"We were almost killed by it," Sarah said solemnly.

Ma jumped, startled.

Abby tried to explain. "We were in a cave near the ocean, and it was a bit scary," she admitted, "but everything turned out all right."

"Is it safe to go there?" Ma questioned, turning to Sulia.

Paloa answered. "I go there often, Mrs. Kendall. It's always been safe for me."

"We probably will not have any more earthquakes for a long time," Sulia said. "They are not common, so I'm sure the children will be all right."

"Where is everyone?" Abby asked, glancing around.

"Your pa and Duncan are down by the lake. They caught a deer and are preparing the meat right now," Ma said, rising. "And I suppose Sulia and I should quit talking and get dinner started."

"Do you want help?" Abby asked.

"You can pick some fresh vegetables from the garden," Sulia suggested.

Sarah stayed with Ma while the others raced out to the side of the house to a fenced-in area. Corn, cabbage, tomatoes, and peppers grew in lush combination. Soon the children returned with their arms full. "I cannot stay late unless I have already asked my father early in the day," Paloa said sadly.

Sulia hugged her. "We will wait for bird's nest soup tomorrow. You ask him if you can stay tomorrow all night, all right?"

Paloa's face brightened. "I will see you tomorrow, then. Good-bye!"

Abby and Luke walked her out the back door. They watched her pull Timor on his leash as she crossed the distant footbridge that spanned the creek to the left of the mansion.

Then Abby and Luke hiked down past the lake, which was surrounded by tall green grass, to the area where Pa and Duncan were working. As they came up, the men were hoisting the gutted deer up in a tall nutmeg tree to drain. Abby knew it was an unpleasant, but necessary, step in preparing the meat for salting and drying. Since they weren't staying long on the island, they would have to finish drying the venison on board the ship.

Pa tied off the load, then joined the kids as they

hiked past a dilapidated warehouse. "Wonder what's in there?" Luke asked.

"Sulia told us that nutmegs were once processed there," Pa explained.

"It looks pretty old and dirty," Abby said.

Luke grinned at her. "Then let's go in and see."

Duncan laughed at Luke. "Thomas and I are going to wash up for dinner. Ye two go ahead if ye want."

"Don't be too long," Pa said as the men headed past them.

Abby watched Luke hike toward the barnlike door of the building. When he reached out to open it, the door swung back with a rusty creak, sending shafts of late-afternoon sunlight into the dark interior. There was a sudden *whoosh,* and black wings flew out through the wide door and broken windows, startling them both.

"Bats!" Luke yelled. At least 100 giant bats flooded the sky around them, darkening the sun momentarily. Their webbed wings seemed huge to Abby.

"Get down," Luke hollered. "They'll get tangled in your hair!"

Abby kneeled and quickly covered her head with her hands. When the noise stopped, she lifted her face.

Luke was grinning. "That was great!" he gushed. "This island is full of surprises." He immediately headed inside.

"Luke!" Irritated, Abby followed him in. It

smelled of musty spice and was full of old crates, old tables, and . . . bat droppings! "Ugh, my shoes."

The scent was strong in the warehouse and, as soon as Abby's eyes adjusted, she could see why. The tables and crates were covered with brownish-red nutmeg powder. They scanned the dim interior and discovered several open boxes of reddish powder. "Looks like this box of spice has bat droppings in it," Abby said. "Too bad it's ruined."

"Hey, look," Luke cried as he hurried forward, investigating ahead of her. "There's a bunch of old ropes," he said, bending over to pick one up. "And look at all the nets in here. Wonder what they used it for." He peered into some crates under one table. "A box of little nuts and a big box of these dried red things," he said, holding up what looked to Abby like shriveled plant roots.

"Let's ask Sulia what this shriveled stuff is," she suggested as they headed out into the blinding sunlight.

They headed back up the hillside toward the mansion. The tropical forest was on their right, the lake on their left. The air was hot and humid with the lazy sound of insects buzzing. Abby felt tired and ready for a rest. Her legs were weary from all the walking, and soon Luke had moved ahead of her. Sarah and Sandy were playing on the back veranda under a small awning, and he hurried to join them.

All alone, Abby was the only one who noticed the

tropical ferns on her right move and jerk. For a moment she thought her eyes had played tricks on her, and she stopped to rub them. When she began walking again, the bushes rustled a second time, as if some animal was behind them. A little spark of fear jolted down her back.

For a second she wondered if some creature was tracking her.

"Hey, wait up!" she cried out, hurrying toward the mansion even as she glanced over her shoulder. The movement had stopped. But her pulse throbbed wildly in her veins. *That's silly; there's nothing here to hurt me,* she told herself.

But her body wasn't listening to reason.

A strong sense of foreboding and a pounding heart told her that danger lurked nearby.

Chapter Five

"This stuff is great," Luke said as he took a second helping of cooked rice and *gado-gado*, which consisted of fresh vegetables smothered in peanut sauce. He speared a red bell pepper and held it up to Abby. "Which pepper always complains about being cold?" he asked, one nut-brown eyebrow raised.

Abby shrugged her shoulders, but Sarah's eyes glowed with interest. "Which one, Luke?" she asked.

"The *chili* pepper, of course!" Luke said with a grin. As soon as he finished eating, he pulled out the red shriveled-up thing he'd found in the warehouse. "Sulia, can you tell me what this is?"

"Mace," Sulia explained. "It comes from the meat of the nutmeg fruit. It's dried for cooking."

Luke held out a small brown nut.

She took it and held it up for all to see. "This is the heart of the nutmeg—the seed," she explained. "It is dried for several weeks, then ground into spice."

"Sulia," Sarah said, withdrawing a small fragrant

43

twig from her pinafore pocket and handing it to her, "what is this?"

"This is from the clove bush. See the flowers? Those are picked and then dried as spice."

Uncle Samuel patted his full tummy and thanked Sulia and Ma for the delicious meal. "Spices and new animals abound on this island," he said with a satisfied sigh. "Lani and I saw some wondrous sights today—bromeliads of all colors— those are flowers that live on tree trunks," he said. "Tomorrow I'd like to take you children with us."

Lani smiled at Uncle Samuel. "You have to see butterfly meadow. Their wings are like rainbows."

"I *have* seen it," Uncle Samuel said dreamily. "Today, with you."

Lani laughed. "I was speaking to the *children*."

He winked at her. "I know, but it's fun to see you blush."

When Abby caught the twinkle in Ma's pretty brown eyes she realized Ma approved of Uncle Samuel's growing friendship with beautiful Lani.

"We saw something really scary in the forest today," Sarah said. "It was a big snakelike thing with scales, and it dropped out of a tree."

Abby nodded at Uncle Samuel, who was sitting up straight and listening. "It looked like a lizard, Uncle Samuel, a really big one. And it was chasing these little monkey creatures called *tarsiers* up in the trees. Then it fell out of the tree by accident. It had this long yellow tongue—forked like a snake's.

44

Paloa said it's called an *ora,* and its bite is poison-ous."

Ma gasped and clutched her throat. Gentle Lani, sitting next to her, patted Ma's shoulder in a comforting manner. Abby glanced her way and immediately wished she'd not made such a big deal of the lizard. Pa was frowning, and Duncan busily twirled his dark handlebar moustache, a sure sign he, too, was concerned.

"You would think a scaly lizard would move slow," Pa commented, "but this one appeared to put up quite a chase of those tarsiers?"

"Yep," Luke said. "It started to come toward us, too, but changed its mind."

Uncle Samuel listened attentively. "You say it had a forked tongue?" he asked Abby.

She nodded.

"Well," he continued, "lizards are cold-blooded, so they usually hunt during the day, after the sun has warmed them. But I imagine if these critters have an acute sense of smell, like a snake does, they would be drawn to the smell of easy prey or rotting meat no matter what time of day it was."

Abby noticed that Sulia was silent during this dinner conversation. Perhaps she didn't go out in the jungle and had never encountered an *ora* before.

After the dinner dishes were done, Sulia showed Abby and Sarah to their upstairs bedroom. "This room has a nice rope bed," she said, pointing, "and it overlooks the lake out back. I hope the jungle noises put you to sleep quickly." She helped Abby make up the bed with a layer of blankets over the ropes and clean sheets over that. Then she smiled at them both. "I am glad you are here to spend time with Paloa."

Sarah and Abby quickly cleaned their hands and faces at the washstand near the window and crawled into bed. Abby's legs ached from her long walk. Soon after she blew out the candle, Sarah fell fast asleep, but Abby could feel the hard ropes through the blanket. She listened to the bird cries and the evening breeze in the trees. They combined to create an exotic song, along with the spicy fragrance that wafted in through the open window. *I love it here,* Abby thought. *Even the air smells delicious.*

She was just drifting off when a loud cracking noise jarred her awake. It sounded like it came from the lake area. *Maybe Pa's splitting wood,* she thought. *But no, he'd wait 'til morning for that chore.* For a moment, she thought she heard a deep growl or hiss, but it could have been the wind. She opened one eye sleepily. Through the open window, she saw that the moon was covered with clouds, and no stars showed through. Abby wanted to get up to see what was making that noise, but she was so tired. *. . . Chances are, I wouldn't be able to see much in the darkness anyway.*

She turned over and fell to sleep.

Gawik! Gawik!

The jarring screech—as loud as a steam whistle—made Abby bolt up in bed. Sarah groaned and buried her head under her pillow. When the cry erupted again, it was so unearthly that Abby threw off the sheet and leapt up. *What on earth is that?*

She threw on her clothes, her green dress that Pa had retrieved with other necessities from the ship, and splashed water on her face at the washstand by the window. Then she flew down the stairs with her hair streaming out behind her. The aroma of strong coffee wafted up to greet her, and Abby suspected Ma was already working in the kitchen.

Sure enough, Ma and Sulia were sipping cups of the brew, again in deep discussion over an opened Bible on the table.

"Excuse me, Ma, but what on earth is that noise?" Abby asked as she padded barefoot across the wood plank flooring.

Sulia grinned. "We call that bird our 'wake up' bird. It's loud, yes?"

Abby shook her head in amazement. "Shockingly loud! Will it do that every morning?"

"I'm afraid so, but at least I never sleep away the day." Sulia actually giggled, and Abby joined her and Ma. Today Sulia looked younger, happier, full of hope. Ma's visit was doing her good.

"Where's Pa this morning?" Abby asked.

Ma wiped a tear of laughter from her eye. "He and Duncan left before sunup to hunt again. They said they'd return soon to start cutting and drying the venison. Thought they might be able to double their supply of it with an early-morning hunt. But Luke just got up and headed out back."

Abby grinned and raced outside to see a few vapors of mist rising off the lake and drifting into the trees. It was still partially shaded. Luke was standing near the large nutmeg trees in the distance. Abby hollered and waved her arm as she headed down the slope toward him. "What's up?" she called cheerfully when she got to him.

"It's not what's up," Luke said. "It's what's come down. The deer's gone."

"Pa and Duncan must have moved it."

"I thought the same thing," Luke said, "until I realized that the tree limb it was hanging from is gone, too. The men would have no reason to tear that limb from the tree." He pointed to the scarred tree trunk where splinters of white wood, the remnants of the limb, were all that was left. "Look at the wound it made when the branch was ripped off."

"Sugar lumps," Abby said, moving closer to study the tree. "Luke," she said, her voice rising with concern, "look at the scratches here on the bark. They're deep and long, like a bowie knife slashed into the tree."

Luke put his hand out to trace one. "Why would

48

someone score the tree with a knife?" he said. "These cuts almost look like claw marks, the way they're evenly spaced. But I didn't think there were any big cats on the island. And frankly, if these are claw marks, then the cat would have to be huge—" he joked now—"as big as a saber-toothed tiger."

Abby brushed her braid off her shoulder. "We better go ask Sulia if there are lions or jungle tigers here." Abby suddenly remembered the ominous feeling she'd had yesterday when she had seen those ferns move—and she'd felt as if she were being watched. The sun dipped behind a cloud and Abby felt her palms grow clammy at the memory. It was as if she had been stalked or hunted!

By the time they returned to the house, however, Sulia and Ma had prepared fresh mango, banana, and papaya for breakfast. Sarah, Uncle Samuel, and Lani had joined them at the dining-room table.

"Sit down, pray, and dig in," Ma ordered in her good-natured way. For the moment, Abby forgot her concerns as she and Luke obeyed Ma's instructions.

It wasn't until after Uncle Samuel and Lani left to gather their things for another forest hike that Abby remembered to question Sulia. "Are there any large cats here?" she asked. "Tigers, maybe?"

"No," Sulia answered, looking baffled.

"How about bears?" Abby said.

"There are bears on Celebes Island but not here. There are many snakes—*ular*—big and small, so keep your eyes open as you go through the forest. Sometimes they drop out of trees."

"Well, if any big snakes drop on our heads," Luke said to Abby as they headed out back, "I have my trusty pocketknife." He held up the four-inch blade. "But I guess I was wrong about those being claw marks—and I'm glad I was. Your pa must've moved the deer."

Relief flooded Abby. "It's the only logical explanation," she agreed. Just like Hawaii, there were no large predators here. Obviously it had only been the wind moving those ferns after all.

"Should we wait for Paloa?" Abby asked Sulia when Uncle Samuel, Lani, and Sarah joined them.

"No, you go on your hike. She knows all this area, and she can take you on another hike tomorrow or later," Sulia said.

Uncle Samuel shouldered a goatskin water bag, and Lani carried a small day sack with snacks in it. "There's something special we want to show you," Lani said as they headed out the back door and past the lake.

Chapter Six

As soon as they got started on their field hike, Uncle Samuel became the biologist-teacher from whom Abby loved to learn.

"Within this forest canopy live a multitude of birds, insects, mammals, and reptiles. Those are starlings," said Uncle Samuel, "and those are small weaver finches." When a larger bird swooped by and caught a dragonfly, he nodded. "And that, as you know, is a dark-feathered crow."

But 40 minutes later, Abby was beginning to wish she hadn't come. Her legs were feeling numb around the ankles, and she was practically tripping over leaves. Luke slowed down and took her elbow to lend her some support as Uncle Samuel, oblivious to her tiredness, pointed out plants that he found fascinating. "So far," he said, "we've seen ironwood trees, rattan, and bamboo. Of course, bamboo is actually a giant grass," Uncle Samuel said enthusiastically, "and we're already familiar with the frangipani tree." He gazed at Lani, then turned back to the path.

Abby had picked a sweet white-yellow blossom from a branch before they entered the forest. Now she took it out of her hair and sniffed it. "Frangipani are my favorite," she said, inhaling the scent.

Lani grinned at her. "All my life plumeria blossoms have been a symbol of home. Maybe tonight we can string some lei. I've been missing my islands."

"I'll help you collect blossoms, Lani," Uncle Samuel said, concerned. She smiled at his blushing face, and he hurried on to change the subject. "That's a bromeliad." He pointed. "It practically grows in the air, see? Lani and I collected four different varieties of them yesterday."

As the two adults moved ahead of them, Abby slowed down to speak to Luke. "Just think," she whispered, "if we hadn't sailed to Hawaii when Uncle Samuel got sick last year, we wouldn't have a shipping business with Duncan, so we wouldn't be here now . . . and my uncle would never have met Lani!"

"So?" Luke said, his forehead creasing.

"Luke," Abby said in exasperation, "it's *so* romantic!"

Luke rolled his eyes. "Abby, sometimes you're such a . . . *a girl!*"

"Thank you," she said, smiling sweetly at him.

"What else would you expect Abby to be?" Sarah complained.

Uncle Samuel now waited on the path for them to catch up. "Well," he said, "we saved the best part for last!" They soon emerged from under the dense forest canopy into a wide-open glade covered with wildflowers of violet, orange, and yellow. Above the meadow flowers floated a thousand sun-drenched butterflies. Their blue-and-purple wings dipped and fluttered on the soft warm breeze.

Sarah was enthralled with the sight. "I'm going to call this place Butterfly Grove," she said.

Uncle Samuel looked pleased, and even Luke began to whisper so he wouldn't disturb the butterflies. "A waterfall," he commented softly, pointing past the meadow to a steep hill of black volcanic rock. A gushing stream tumbled down the rock face, splashed into a dark pool beneath, and traveled on in a stream to their far left.

"That's where the creek by the mansion comes from," Uncle Samuel explained. "It runs over that way, close to the path but not beside it."

As they walked in the sun through the open meadow, they noted that torches were stuck in the ground in various places. "Apparently," Uncle Samuel said, "the islanders come here at night."

"What is that, Uncle Samuel?" Luke asked, coming up to many large black rocks piled about waist high around the pool. "These are volcanic rocks, aren't they? I recognize them from Hawaii."

On top of the black porous rocks was a wide, white stone. On it lay strewn flowers, now dead. There were also banana leaves and dark brown stains.

"You're right, Luke. I believe this stone is used to

pay tribute to the gods of these islanders," Uncle Samuel responded.

Lani nodded. "It reminds me of places in Hawaii," she agreed. "No doubt these dead flowers were brought here when they were fresh and beautiful, but they've since wilted. And the banana leaves probably held food as an offering. They must believe that this is where the volcano god lives, since we are at the foot of the volcano."

"What's this dark brown stuff on the white stone?" Abby said.

Uncle Samuel pursed his lips together. "Those are bloodstains, I'm afraid. Some animal lost its life here."

Sarah swallowed. "Better keep Sandy in the house unless we're with her!"

"You never know what you'll find in the remote parts of the earth," Uncle Samuel said.

"After all," Luke teased, his voice dropping ominously low and threatening, "the map said, *Here Be Dragons.*"

Abby slugged him playfully and sat down on a boulder. "Well, it's one more thing to put in my report for Ma." She gazed at the hundreds of butterflies fluttering on the warm air above a thousand flowers. "It's like they're dancing to music we can't hear."

"Fanciful thinking," Uncle Samuel said with a smile. "Shall we go?"

"Let's eat first," Luke said.

"A picnic!" Sarah agreed as Lani sat down on the rock and dug into the day pack.

Abby gazed up at them with relief. Luke's ever-hungry stomach would give her legs a much-needed rest.

A while later Uncle Samuel led them off the beaten track to show them something he considered "unusual." A short distance from the pool were several three-foot-high "mud mountains," he explained.

"We are very close to the volcano," he said, becoming the teacher again, "and obviously it has several vents to release the pressure mounting in it. These mud volcanoes look like tiny volcanoes, but they erupt with mud instead of lava. They're allowing the volcano to vent some steam or gas."

Sarah and Luke watched in fascination as the small mud volcanoes bubbled with brown goo. The hot mud came out the tops and spilled over the sides of the little mountains it was forming.

Abby grew bored before the others and wandered off to a nearby outcropping of rocks. "Hey," she shouted, "I found a cave entrance."

Luke jumped up and followed her. The others were close behind. Abby pointed to a wide-open cave that was recessed below ground.

"I wonder where it goes," Luke said, jumping past Abby down several feet to the cave opening. He stepped in a few feet, then called out, "It's too dark to see anything." Climbing back up, he stood beside the others. "But I know how to fix that." He raced off and returned quickly with a torch from the sacrificial area.

Uncle Samuel grinned as Luke dug in his pockets for some of the sputtering matches he'd gotten in China. Soon the torch was flaring, and Luke urged everyone to follow him.

"No sir!" Sarah objected. "Last time I went in a scary tunnel, we had a big earthquake."

"What are the chances that will happen again?" Luke reasoned.

"There's no chance it'll happen again," Sarah said, "if I don't go inside."

Luke's face puckered into a frown, and he sat down on a nearby boulder. Sarah came close to say she was sorry but accidentally knocked his hold on the lit torch. It fell six feet down and landed at the cave entrance, lighting up the shadows. Luke glanced down at it and groaned. "Now you've gone and done it, short stuff." He got up to fetch it when Abby gasped.

"What's that stuff moving down there?" she asked.

Lani peered over her shoulder. "Oh, goodness! Those are scorpions on the ground."

"Nightmares!" Sarah shrieked. "I don't like caves; I don't like them at all!"

Lani nodded. "It would take an exploding volcano for me to go down there," she vowed. "Let's leave the torch and go."

Abby decided that Lani was not only beautiful, but smart. Her absentminded uncle should definitely marry her. Soon.

Chapter Seven

Sarah, with her quick eyes, was the first to notice Paloa, Timor, and Sandy on the back porch. She waved and yelled a greeting, and Sandy bounded down the incline to greet them. Her tail wagging for joy, she leapt up on Sarah and licked her hand.

Paloa's white teeth showed as she welcomed them back. "You look hot and tired. How about going for a swim?"

"It's hot enough to fry eggs on rocks," Luke said. "I'm game."

The very idea of sinking in cool water sounded heavenly to Abby.

Paloa ushered them into the kitchen and asked her grandmother about extra clothes. "Aren't there some old things in the bedroom dressers they could use to swim in, Grandmother, so their clothes won't get wet?"

"Yes," Sulia said, "please help them find things. And children, keep your eyes open for water snakes and pythons."

Abby paused. Maybe this wasn't such a great

idea. Hawaii had few dangerous animals to worry about, and the only snakes there were sea snakes. But the heat was miserable. She decided she'd risk snakes to cool off.

Paloa eagerly motioned for them to follow her. They all hurried upstairs and entered Abby and Sarah's room. Paloa went to the wooden dresser and pulled out drawers, searching through old clothes. Lifting up several things, Abby saw they were all in the same type of cotton print that Sulia and Paloa wore.

"I love this material," Abby said, kneeling down next to Paloa. "The pattern is different than any I've seen."

"We call this *batik*. It's dyed a special way," Paloa explained. "First we put hot wax on the cloth in a pattern. Then we dye it. When it's dry, we take off the wax and it's white where the wax had been. But for our special feasts and dances, we wear bright silk sarongs." She handed Abby and Sarah each a calf-length skirt and sleeveless blouse. "This will be much easier to move in—and cooler," she said. "You two get dressed, and I'll show Luke something from his room."

The girls quickly dressed in the lightweight clothes and left their shoes under the bed, but a movement under the bed made Abby scream and push herself backward.

Two little gray mice scurried out from their hiding place and raced right over Abby's bare toes.

"Arrgghh!" Abby jumped up, terrified. The mice, apparently just as scared as Abby, bounded toward a tiny hole in the wall and disappeared.

Footsteps pounded in the hallway, and Luke burst into the room. "What's wrong?"

When Abby turned to tell him, she couldn't get the words out. He was wearing a skirt just like hers. "You're wearing girl clothes!" she gasped.

Luke drew himself up, crossing his arms defensively. "Paloa says all the men dress like this. Even her father, the headman of the village. And Duncan once told me all the great Scottish warriors wear kilts—much shorter skirts than this one."

Abby bit her lip to keep from laughing at the *batik* cotton sarong and Luke's tanned calves sticking out below it. But Sarah didn't try to hide her delight. She simply doubled over with giggles.

Luke stomped off barefoot. "I'm heading down to the lake. Paloa's waiting."

"Oops," Abby said. "We better go make up." The girls hurried down the stairs after him. Together they found Paloa already at the water.

She smiled as they came up. "No snakes," Paloa said happily. "Except for many frogs and fish, the lake is all ours."

Soon they were splashing each other in the shallows and swimming in deeper water. "The water feels heavenly in this heat," Abby said. While attempting to catch a fat fish with his hands, Luke went underwater and came up with pond algae on his head. Laughter rang out.

"Paloa," Abby said much later, as they left Sarah and Luke to play in the water while they sat in the sun to dry, "it's great having another girl around. Do you want to join our ship and become a sailor?"

Paloa's silky black hair draped over her shoulders and glistened in the sun. "Oh no. Grandmother's heart would break if I left. She's already so lonely," she said, shaking her head sadly. "I try to be a whole family for her, but I can't replace village life."

Abby sobered at her words. "Isn't there any hope that Sulia and Kaliman can make up?"

"My father used to come once or twice a year to check on her . . . you know, to fix things that had broken or to bring a large fish he'd caught. But two years ago he became very angry for some reason. He wouldn't tell me, but he's never been back."

Abby sighed. "I guess it's good that we're staying awhile, so Ma can visit with her."

Paloa nodded. "Yes, I'm thankful God's brought all of you. And I pray that somehow, someday, God will change my father's heart." Paloa turned to study her hands, as if there were some message to read there.

Seeing that Paloa's pretty, almond-shaped eyes were bright with tears, Abby reached out to pat Paloa's back. "I'll pray for them. I've seen God do a lot of things that looked impossible. Once Luke and I were captured by a pirate, and God rescued us."

Paloa glanced up. "Truly?"

Abby nodded. "Another time we were thrown overboard and got lost at sea, but God kept us safe. Nothing's impossible for Him."

Paloa turned her head away and wiped at the tears.

Nothing's impossible, Abby thought, *but sometimes people have to be willing to listen to God's voice for the miracle to happen.*

I know Sulia is listening, she thought, *but is Kaliman?*

The kids were just getting ready to head up the slope to the mansion when Pa and Duncan emerged from the forest, shotguns over their shoulders and each man holding a quail.

"Dinner!" Pa shouted to Abby and Sarah as he held up his catch.

He and Duncan came toward them, but Duncan stopped suddenly. "Thomas!" he exclaimed. "Where's the buck we had hanging there?"

Abby's eyes met Luke's.

"We thought *you* moved it," Luke said as he came toward the men.

"Nay." Duncan scowled.

It was then that Abby remembered the noises she'd heard last night, the sound like wood splitting. She suddenly realized it must have been the tree branch splitting. She quickly told Pa and Duncan about it.

"Did you get a look at who took it?" Pa questioned.

Abby felt that she'd let him down. "I'm sorry, Pa. I didn't think about the meat then, so I didn't go look."

Pa let out a sigh of exasperation. "It's not your fault, Princess. It must have been too great a temptation for someone. . . . Maybe some boys came and stole it." He punched the toe of his boot into the soft earth over and over. Abby knew he was trying to calm down.

"That's not fair," Sarah said, crossing her arms. "You want me and Luke to go look for it, Pa? I can tell that Abby's legs are tired, but Duncan—he's a private investigator—could come, too. He's good at solving mysteries."

Pa grinned. "No, Little Britches. We'll thank God for a quail dinner tonight and hope we can get venison tomorrow."

"Mr. Kendall," Paloa said softly, "my village is small. I will know if anyone has brought home a buck recently. I can check for you."

Pa thanked her as they hiked toward the mansion.

"And next time," Duncan said, "we won't leave it unguarrrded."

The fried quail tasted delicious over rice cooked in sweet coconut milk. There were crispy cucumbers and plump red tomatoes, too. Abby was surprised that Sulia's garden, on an exotic island in the Banda Sea, had many of the same vegetables that their garden in Pueblo de San Jose, California, had.

After the meal, they sat on the back veranda in the dusky light while Uncle Samuel played his guitar and sang "Turkey in the Straw" and "Yankee Doodle," both new tunes to Sulia and Paloa. Soon darkness fell, however, and the stars shone like glittering diamonds.

The distant sound of the jungle and the closer chorus of frogs and crickets created a soothing melody. Ma finally sent the children upstairs to sleep, and Paloa made her bed on the downstairs bench with the worn-out pillows, since her father had given her permission to stay the night.

"Tomorrow will be a fun day together," Abby promised Paloa as she leaned over the banister. She watched Paloa snuggle under her sheet. Mr. Looloo, the tailless ape, settled in an armchair, and sweet little Timor lay down at Paloa's feet, as faithful a pet as any dog could be.

Chapter Eight

More annoying than any rooster's crowing, the cry of the "wake up" bird split Abby's ears early the next morning. She groaned and lay in bed for a few more minutes, listening to it croak out an unearthly greeting. Surely its cry must reach other islands in the Banda Sea!

Sarah burrowed under her pillow again with a sleepy sigh.

Before long, however, the whole family was up and dressed. After a breakfast of sweet melons and coconut rice, the kids wandered out back.

Abby turned eagerly to Paloa. "Would you show us your village?" she asked. She wanted a close-up look at that village they'd sailed past, and maybe Paloa could learn if anyone had stolen Pa's deer meat.

"That sounds fun," Sarah said. "We could see your house."

"But I was hoping for a special tour of the forest," Luke objected.

"We must pass through some of the forest to get to my village," Paloa said, but she looked at Abby hesitantly.

"What is it?" Abby saw that something about going to her village bothered their new friend.

Paloa frowned. "I'm sorry, but my father won't be happy if I bring you into our village. It will cause a big commotion because people will want to celebrate your arrival. Many people will want to come here to the mansion to visit you because you are foreigners . . . and, well, Father doesn't want people out here visiting Grandmother. He wants Grandmother to come home to live at the village." Paloa hesitated, then continued. "My father, Kaliman, is a good man, but very stub-born sometimes!" She looked glum and hopeless.

"I understand," Abby said, nodding in sympathy. "What if we hike through the forest and peek at your village so I can write about it in the school report Ma's making me do? Then later we can go on a longer hike in the forest for Luke?"

Paloa grinned. "Yes! That's a good idea. Come on!" she said, pulling Timor on his leash.

Tying a leash on Sandy, they retraced Paloa's trail over the footbridge and followed the tropical forest path, well trod by Paloa's daily visits to the mansion.

It wasn't more than two miles along the coast and sometimes through the forest before the children reached a rise that overlooked the village.

Ahead of them lay a wide-open space where jungle had been cleared. The village sat overlooking the Banda Sea to the left. Abby could see the white-sand beach and distant blue water. Many small wooden boats were moored on a few rickety-looking docks that jutted out over very shallow waters. She could tell it was shallow because of the pale blue color. Behind the village the forest rose up, and in the distance, the tall mountain crouched, casting a late-morning shadow over the land.

Many bamboo homes sat on stilts. Abby spied a catlike animal sleeping in the sun on top of a roof. "Is that a cat?" she asked.

"No, that is a *musang*," Paloa said. "It lives in palm trees or on rooftops. People are glad to have them because they eat many insects—even scorpions."

Abby shuddered at the thought of so many poisonous snakes and bugs thriving on this steamy tropical island. She'd never seen a scorpion in Hawaii, although she had encountered a poisonous orange centipede.

Children were running everywhere, laughing and playing tag. Goats, pigs, and chickens either grazed the pockets of grass around the village or were tethered near family homes. A few of the animals yanked on their ropes, as if trying to get away.

Abby didn't speak but silently took in the scene, watching women busy themselves over outdoor cook fires, talking together as they stirred pots. *Perhaps preparing the next meal,* Abby thought.

"Where is your house?" Sarah whispered to Paloa.

"Next to that man herding pigs out of the village," she answered.

"Is your father here?" Luke asked.

"He should be, but I don't see him yet," Paloa said, scanning the scene. "He might have gone to visit—"

But Paloa never finished her thought because just then the earth trembled violently, throwing her onto Sarah. Sandy barked in fear, and Abby stumbled and fell to the ground. Luke gripped a sturdy bamboo as the shaking continued for what seemed like ages but was really only seconds longer.

As soon as the ground stopped pitching and rolling, wailing sounds erupted from the village—screams and cries of fear. Abby pushed herself up and helped Sarah while Luke lifted Paloa from the ground where she'd sprawled.

Sarah's slate-blue eyes were wide as she clung to Abby. "That was a giant earthquake!"

Paloa wiped the dirt off her hands and peered at her village. "That fallen house belongs to my friend." Abby followed her pointing, and saw that, indeed, two bamboo houses had slid off their meager foundations and lay at odd angles. "I must help," Paloa said.

As she sprinted toward the home with Timor flying behind her, Luke caught Abby's eye. "We should see if we can do anything," he said. Abby

70

nodded, and the three followed Paloa into the village. A muscular man hurried toward Paloa, shouting in a strange language.

He intercepted Paloa and hugged her tightly. In a moment Luke, Sarah, and Abby caught up to them.

Luke leaned over and whispered to Abby, "I'm glad to see he's wearing a skirt, too."

Kaliman's dark eyes raked over them. A scowl formed as he turned to Paloa and spoke in their language.

"Boy, their language sounds hard to learn," Luke whispered.

Paloa heard Luke's comment and shook her head. "Not nearly so hard as English! But Father knows a little English, too, from his work on the plantation." She turned back to him and spoke slowly and respectfully. "Father, this is Abby and Sarah Kendall and Luke Quiggley. Their parents sailed into Grandmother's bay, and they are staying at the mansion." She turned slightly to the children and said, "This is Kaliman, my father, the headman of our village."

Luke reached out a hand to shake, and Kaliman took it, staring him squarely in the eye. "You are welcome," he said gruffly. He gave a rough small smile to Abby and Sarah. "I must help now." And with that he left them.

Luke instantly followed him and set to work helping him lift bamboo logs that had fallen. Paloa's face had paled, and Abby took her hand. "We'll stay and help."

Abby and Sarah followed Paloa as she moved through the village, speaking in her native tongue, checking on each family. Together the girls helped several families set their homes to right. When they checked on Paloa's home, nothing had been greatly hurt, but items had been wildly tossed around.

"Everyone is safe," Paloa said with relief an hour later. "Normally, my people would make you feel very welcome with food and songs, but today things are not normal."

Luke, who had just joined them, nodded. "It's okay. We were glad to help, but we need to get back in case Abby's mom is worried."

"You're right, Luke," Abby said, giving Paloa a hug. "You stay here, but maybe you can join us later at the mansion?"

"I'll try," Paloa said. "Just stay on the path—it leads straight back to Grandmother's."

As they retraced their steps, Sarah complained about the heat. Though not even noon, the day was muggy and sweat trickled down their backs and foreheads. Poor little Sandy seemed to be dragging, too. When they emerged along an ocean cliff again, a cooler breeze hit their thankful faces.

The mansion was now in sight. Because of Ma's assignment, Abby couldn't help comparing this island to her beloved Hawaiian Islands. *It's hotter here, there are too many poisonous snakes and bugs . . . and I'm not fond of the way the way the ground rearranges itself without warning!*

Chapter Nine

As Abby, Luke, and Sarah crossed the footbridge
and headed toward the back of the house, they
could hear Ma and Pa talking on the outside porch.
It was apparent Ma had been worried about them
ever since the earthquake had shaken the mansion.
She rushed toward them to make sure they were all
in one piece, then insisted they sit on the back
veranda and have lunch at the table with Pa and
Duncan, who'd returned empty-handed from hunting.

As soon as the meal ended, Abby set to work in
her journal, making notes of their morning walk
and Paloa's village. It also gave her a reason to rest
her legs. She was busy drawing a picture of the flowered lianas, the vines hanging down from the forest
canopy, when Luke interrupted her.

"Can't you write tonight, Abby?" Luke asked.
"The day is getting away from us. I'd like to go for
another hike—or maybe a swim."

"Just a few more minutes," she said. Even though
Luke understood about her weak legs, she hated to

talk about them unless she had to. Soon she slapped her journal shut and went to change into her borrowed clothes.

"Let's swim," she said as she descended the stairs. Luke and Sarah were playing cards in the parlor, and they both looked up.

Luke's cheek dimpled. "Yee-haw!" he shouted, taking the stairs two at a time and flying by her so fast she caught a cool breeze. Sarah buzzed on by like a busy bee, too, and five minutes later they were heading down the slope to the lake.

They hurried to the lake and enjoyed a long cool swim in the water until the sky darkened with gathering thunderclouds.

"Abby," Luke said, eyeing the turbulent sky that was blowing in from the sea, "we should probably head back in now."

She sighed and climbed out of the water. "Come on, Sarah. Time to go."

"Just a bit more," Sarah said, diving under the water again.

Luke tossed a pebble into the lake's center, then glanced skyward at the dark clouds boiling overhead. "I'm heading up to the house. Don't let Sarah stay too long—there could be lightning coming."

Abby nodded. "Come on, slowpoke!" she called

to Sarah as she shook out the towel she'd brought down. Sarah played another minute, while Abby retrieved Sarah's towel and headed toward her just as she emerged, dripping, from the water. "It's cool and refreshing, huh?" she said while patting Sarah's shoulders dry.

"That water feels good," Sarah said happily. Then, suddenly, her face drained of color. Panic skittered across her features.

Abby turned to see what was frightening her, and her legs instantly felt like mush.

Out of the brush, only 20 yards away, appeared—

A crocodile, an alligator! Abby's mind churned to understand what she was seeing. *No—an ora!*

The lizard was as big as a grizzly! Horror shot through Abby like a lightning bolt. This *ora* was identical to the one she'd seen in the forest, but it was 10 feet long! And it was coming straight toward them, its yellow tongue flicking in and out rapidly as its head swung back and forth.

Abby could feel Sarah tremble violently, yet she was rooted to the spot in terror. Her stomach clutched into a cold ball. But as Sarah let out a bloodcurdling scream, Abby was shocked into action. She grabbed Sarah's arm in a death grip and yanked her toward the mansion, flying as fast as her slow legs could go.

Abby gasped in panic. She didn't dare turn to see if the dragon was stampeding after them. Not until they hit the veranda and flew into the kitchen did

Abby turn and look back as they hurried past Luke, who sat at the kitchen table.

Ma, having heard Sarah's scream, ran down the stairs and into the kitchen just as Abby got Sarah to the dining room.

"What is it?" Ma asked, kneeling in front of Sarah and embracing her.

"M-m-m-monster," Sarah stuttered, and tears began to fall.

Sulia hurried toward them from the hallway and met Abby's gaze with a stricken look. "A dragon? An *ora?*" she asked. Abby nodded silently.

All at once Luke was there, too, questions flying. Abby, too shaken to talk much, said simply, "Come see for yourself."

But when they all rushed through the back door and onto the porch, there was no sign of the monster anywhere.

"It was there," Abby insisted, pointing toward the water. But she wasn't sure Luke believed her.

"Was it like the one we saw yesterday?" he asked quizzically.

"No! Sarah wouldn't have been that frightened by a little *ora*—that was nothing compared to this one. This dragon was huge, as big as a grizzly bear on all fours!"

Luke, who'd faced a grizzly attack in California, looked skeptical. "I'll go down and check for prints," he said, but Sarah shrieked in fear.

"N-n-n-no!" she said adamantly. "It will eat you up."

Ma's eyes narrowed in concern, but Luke just patted Sarah gently on the back. "All right, short stuff. I'll stay here."

Sulia urged them to come back into the house. "Why don't we go up to the attic and take your mind off dragons for a bit?" she asked kindly.

Sarah's face was still ashen, and she gripped Ma's hand. "No. I want to stay with Ma."

Ma put an arm around her to comfort her. "Why don't you help me test the banana pudding I'm making, sweetheart?" Together she and Sarah turned toward the stove as Luke took one last look out the door. Then he followed Abby and Sulia out of the kitchen.

"Are you sure," he questioned on their way through the dining room, "that it was really that big? Abby, you sure you haven't been drinking too much hibiscus tea lately?"

Abby's eyes sparked with anger. "Luke Quiggley, I did too see a dragon, a real living dragon. What will it take for you to believe me?"

But Luke was already heading up the stairs, shaking his head as if the whole thing were unbelievable.

Sulia put out a hand to stop Abby. "I believe you, Abby. This island has many strange animals on it. But I have never known an *ora* to come so close to the mansion before," she said unhappily. "I don't know what it means. Earthquakes keep coming, and now an *ora*." Her brows furrowed, and she was about to say more when Paloa opened the kitchen door.

"Grandmother?" Paloa asked, evidently noting Sulia's unhappy expression.

"The earthquake?" Sulia replied quickly.

"The village is fine—two houses damaged, but they are being repaired right now. No one was hurt."

"Thank God," Sulia said, sighing with relief. "He answered my prayers. Why don't we head up to the attic—to take our minds off things? There are secrets in the attic I've never shown you, Paloa."

Instantly interested, both girls climbed the first flight of stairs behind Sulia. They reached the attic just as the downpour started. The house darkened immediately as the black clouds blocked the sun.

Luke had already found a couple of candles and lit them with his matches. Shadows danced as the flames tossed in a slight breeze that came through cracks in the walls. Paloa was bent over an opened trunk, searching through it and pulling out clothing.

Sulia joined her. "This is Mrs. Cleets's trunk. She left some things she no longer wanted," she explained. Moving on, she located another wooden trunk. "Here it is!" she said joyfully. "Ahh, this brings me good memories." She opened the lid and laid it back, then removed a flat, two-dimensional leather puppet with moving arms and legs. It was mounted on bamboo sticks and basically looked like a silhouette, rather than a regular three-dimensional puppet with round head and body.

"This will do beautifully," Sulia said. "I remember putting on performances for Kaliman when he and his friends were little many years ago. The *wayang* stories are still here," she claimed, tapping her forehead with a grin.

"You will put on a puppet show for us?" Abby and Paloa asked at the same time. They looked at each other and giggled. Paloa helped her grandmother remove four more puppets and a big white sheet from the bottom of the trunk.

"Oh, Abby, you will love the *wayang*," Paloa said, excited. "I have seen it in my village and it's fun. Grandmother, can I help you do it?"

Sulia smiled softly at her. "Yes, yes. That will be nice." She seemed to be thinking back to another, happier time, Abby realized.

Abby dug through the other trunk while Luke ambled around, inspecting the old furniture stored against one wall. He found an old wall clock and wound it with a key found under its cover.

Abby, meanwhile, bent over Mrs. Cleets's trunk and pulled out a leather box. She held it up for Sulia to see. "May I look inside this?"

"Yes. Mrs. Cleets only left behind the things she no longer wanted. So you children may take anything you want." When Abby opened the box she was delighted to find an old tortoise comb, three hair ribbons of faded blue and violet, a few Indonesian shell trinkets, and some folded yellowed paper that still carried a slight floral scent.

Sulia wandered over to see what she had found. "Ah, I remember packing this away. I couldn't bear to throw anything out. You see, I loved Mrs. Cleets like a mother. She taught me everything I know about God. I tried to teach my son these truths when he was young, but his father did not believe. He died long ago. So Kaliman, my son, could never decide. He was never fully convinced. I can't help but wonder if he still remembers my teaching. . . ."

"Grandmother," Paloa said, coming to stand beside her, "I believe." She hugged her bent little grandmother, and Sulia's wrinkled face smiled again.

"Now," Paloa said, "why don't we go downstairs and practice a puppet show for tonight? We can entertain Abby's family with a traditional story."

"Yes, of course," Sulia said, handing Paloa several puppets to carry. "You and Luke have fun looking through the attic," she urged as she and Paloa headed down the attic stairs.

Chapter Ten

Sarah had finally calmed down and stopped clinging to Ma by the time Luke and Abby descended from the attic. Abby stored the leather box in her room since she wanted to read the papers and letters later. Then she took Sarah by the hand, trying to encourage her. "Come out on the porch and see the pretty rainbow over the forest."

Against a dark cloud, a brightly colored rainbow spanned the sky. As Abby, Ma, Sarah, and Luke watched it, they spied Lani and Uncle Samuel coming from a forest path toward the mansion. They were laughing and holding hands. Uncle Samuel held a wide banana leaf over Lani's head in an attempt to protect her from the slight rain that still came down, but they were both spotted with raindrops that had made it through the forest canopy.

Pa and Duncan came from the front of the mansion at that moment. They'd been checking on the ship, they explained, and reported that it was still properly anchored and secure.

As Lani and Uncle Samuel stomped onto the veranda, Ma and Pa greeted them. The biologist and beautiful half-Hawaiian woman glowed with happiness.

When they hurried inside to change into dry clothes, Ma pinned Pa with a knowing stare. "I remember when you used to look at me like that."

Pa grinned at her and shook his head. "You mean all twitterpated?" he quipped. "Poor Samuel, it's pert' near fatal." Ma started to whip him with the kitchen towel she was holding but he was too quick for her. He grabbed her and gave her a resounding kiss in front of Abby, Luke, and Sarah.

"Yuck!" Sarah said, turning away. But Pa just reached out and ruffled Sarah's cornsilk hair.

"So," Pa said, turning to Abby, "did you do anything exciting today?"

Ma stepped close to Pa and shook her head no, as she glanced at Sarah. "I think we'll save that discussion until after the children go to bed tonight, Thomas."

Pa got the hint, but his eyebrows raised in curiosity. "Sounds fair," he commented. "Then let's talk about dinner! What are you going to feed me and Luke?" he said with a wink at the youngest man in the family. "We're still growing boys, you know."

"Bird's nest soup?" Luke asked weakly.

"Oh yes!" Paloa said. "A rare treat." She ladled a large portion of it into Luke's bowl.

Abby had to bite her lip to keep from laughing. Sulia and Paloa were eager to share this "treat" with them. If they didn't eat it, wouldn't that be rude and ungrateful?

Paloa grinned at Abby as she came next to her and poured a ladleful into her empty bowl. "Thank you," Abby said, glancing at Luke. He was turning green around the gills.

Pa and Duncan came in from washing up at the outdoor pump. "Mmm," Pa said enthusiastically, "something smells good."

"It's an Indonesian specialty," Sulia said proudly, "and very rare to find all the right ingredients."

Sarah leaned toward Abby and whispered, "Of course it's hard to get all the ingredients! Whoever heard of eating bird eggs *and* the house they live in?"

"Yes," Sulia went on to explain to Samuel and Lani. "It is the bird's saliva that gives it the special flavor."

"Saliva?" Uncle Samuel said. Abby could see that he wasn't sure if she was joking or not.

"Right," Paloa answered. "The bird's spit holds the nest together—sort of like glue—so we boil the whole thing in a big pot. . . ."

She went around the table and finished pouring soup for everyone. Ma gazed down into her bowl. When she glanced up, Abby saw that she looked pale.

Duncan bowed his head and said grace. "We

thank Ye, Lord God, for this grrracious hostess and our time on this island. We prrray, verrry harrrd, that Ye'll keep us all safe and sound. Amen. Well, we've prayed and now it's time to eat our vittles," he said sheepishly. With that he was the first to spoon into the bird's nest soup. Sulia and Paloa watched eagerly as the liquid entered his mouth. The rest of the family held their breath.

Duncan swallowed, then set down his spoon and wiped his moustache. Looking up at Sulia, he nodded thoughtfully. "An interesting flavor!"

Sulia and Paloa smiled broadly while Duncan turned his piercing gray eye on the others. "Dig in," he said.

Everyone dipped their spoons, trying to avoid the pieces of unknown things floating in their bowls. Pa took a deep breath and swallowed his first taste. "Mmm-hmm," he murmured. "It *is* interesting!"

Ma gave Abby and Sarah a stern look. *Oh well,* Abby thought, *no one else has keeled over dead yet.* She sipped a bit off her spoon. It was passable— salty with a bit of an egg flavor and other flavors she couldn't identify.

Sarah, however, just stirred her spoon around and around until the next course of cheese, corn mush, and beans was served. Banana pudding for dessert filled even Luke to the brim.

While the adults sipped their after-dinner coffee, Luke helped Sulia string up a white sheet in the parlor. Two lanterns were taken behind the sheet, and Sarah could hardly wait until the show began.

"But, Abby," Sarah said with a creased forehead, "the sheet is in the way. How will we see the puppets?"

"I don't know. We'll have to wait and find out," she answered.

"I don't like waiting," Sarah whispered.

"You can help me wash dishes until it's time— that way you won't be bored," Abby said with a mischievous grin.

As soon as the last dish had been dried, Paloa ran to get the girls. "We're ready!" Then she hurried to join Sulia.

Luke had arranged chairs to face the white sheet. And now that it was dark outside, the lanterns sitting on tables behind the sheet lit it to a glowing white. Abby could see Sulia's head outlined at the bottom of the sheet. Apparently she and Paloa were now seated on the floor with the lanterns on a table behind them.

Bells tinkled and Sulia's voice called out, "Here is the ancient tale of Ramayana," she said, "and the story of the brave Prince Rama. He fought the evil Ravana with courage!"

A shadow of the first puppet appeared on the white sheet, and Sarah burst into delighted applause. "I see a man!" she said.

"Rama was a prince in the court at Ayutthaya," Sulia began. "He was a good boy and handsome to all the maidens' eyes!" Now the puppet danced and bowed, bells around its feet jingling with music.

"But this good prince was driven from the palace by Ravana, an evil dragon. . . ." On the sheet a dragon appeared. Luke hissed and booed, bringing peals of laughter from Sarah. "Everyone thought that Ravana was a smart magician, but only the good prince knew he was a dragon in disguise.

"When Ravana told evil lies about Prince Rama, the prince was forced to flee his only home, the palace.

"So he ran to the forest where the bamboo grows and the lianas swing." Now the puppet looked like it was running. Then a woman and another man puppet appeared on the screen.

"Prince Rama had a pretty wife, Sita, and a faithful brother, Laksmana. They both followed him because they loved him. They were the only ones who believed Prince Rama was innocent.

"But . . ." Now a drumroll sounded from behind the sheet. "Before Sita could join Prince Rama in the forest, the evil dragon Ravana kidnapped her!" The dragon shadow grabbed the wife puppet with its long claws and dragged her off the stage.

Abby watched Sarah's mouth pucker into a frown. She hoped the story had a happy ending.

"Prince Rama and his brother hurried to get help from the forest animals. They met the monkey king, Sugriva, who offered to support Prince Rama in his fight against the evil dragon." The dark shadow of a

crowned monkey jumped up and down, and everyone laughed.

"Other forest animals helped as well—the tiger,
the bear, and the ox all joined together to fight the
darkness that had settled over the forest lands. They
wanted to help Prince Rama win back his beloved
wife.

"A terrible battle was fought. The birds dropped
stones on Ravana's head. The monkeys screeched
loudly to confuse him. The bear remembered a net
had once caught his friend, and he laid out a net
from a fishing village. But Ravana's sharp teeth
ripped through it. Even the strong oxen with their
horns did their best to swipe at the evil dragon, but
he could not be killed!

"Prince Rama knew that he alone held the only
weapon that could win his wife back. He alone must
kill the dragon with his special knife—the wavy-
bladed *kris*, which he believed had magical powers."
Now the shadow puppet Prince Rama held a wavy-
bladed knife up in the air.

"According to tradition, Prince Rama knew this
ancient *kris* had power enough to fly through the air
and find its target. Prince Rama believed the blade
had been forged by ancient gods for this very
purpose, to balance the forces of good and evil on
the earth. So he let loose the *kris*—and it flew!"

Now the shadow of the *kris* appeared on the
sheet, flying through the air. Abby could easily see

the thin rod that held it aloft, but she enjoyed the story anyway.

"The *kris* flew straight into the heart of the evil Ravana, killing him dead!" The dragon shadow fell when the *kris* hit its chest. Everyone cheered and clapped.

"And Prince Rama ran to rescue his wife, Sita." The two puppets embraced. "Then the three returned, triumphant, to the palace. And Prince Rama was crowned king!" The shadow of his wife holding a crown came toward the prince. She set the crown upon his head, and bells jingled from behind the screen.

"The moral of this story," the king's shadow said, "is that good triumphs over evil."

Everyone clapped again as Sulia and Paloa came out from behind the sheet. They bowed and smiled shyly, apparently pleased that their audience was happy. Then Sulia cleared her throat and all grew quiet. "Although that is an ancient folk legend of my people, I believe that good does triumph over evil. Not because of a magic *kris*, but because of God."

Sarah jumped up. "That's right! Pa and Abby won against the Chinese pirate Zai Ching without any knives or weapons at all—so it had to be God."

Duncan stroked his moustache thoughtfully. "Yerrr right, sweet lassie. We owe our friendship and our business to God, too. Why, if Abby hadn't found me da's diary, I would not have found me sister, Lani. And if me da hadn't carved a dolphin, we might not have escaped with our lives and ship from the pirate king in China. It's easy to see that all along the way, God has ordered our steps. We could not have planned it out so well!"

Abby grinned at Duncan, whose faith had always encouraged her. For a brief moment, she wondered what steps she would be taking that God had already planned out for her.

"Tomorrow night," she said, "Sarah and I will plan a puppet show." Tonight's play had prompted her to think about a story she wanted to share. "We'll practice tomorrow," she told Sarah.

"I must go now, before it grows later," Paloa said. "Or Father will worry about me."

Sarah's face fell at those words. "Don't go out there," she warned. Her distress made it clear she was thinking of the giant dragon. Abby glanced at Sulia and saw concern etched on the old woman's face, too.

"Duncan and I will walk Paloa back to her village," Pa said kindly. "I don't want you out alone in the dark," he explained to Paloa.

Sarah threw herself into Pa's lap. "Don't go, Pa. You don't know what's out there."

"It's all right, honey," he said. "Duncan and I have rifles to kill any beasts that threaten us."

"And we'll carry torches, Sarah," Paloa said.

Sulia reached out a veined hand and put it on

Pa's large one. "Thank you," she said. "I feel better knowing she will be protected."

After they left, Sarah headed up the stairs with a candle in hand. Abby was at the dining-room table going through the puppets. An idea was forming for her own puppet show.

"Are you coming up soon?" Sarah asked.

"In a minute," she replied. She could hear Sulia and Ma talking as they finished chores in the kitchen.

A pot clanged, then Ma's voice spoke. "And why doesn't your son ever come to visit?" Abby heard Ma ask.

"He used to visit a couple of times a year," Sulia's quiet voice answered. "But two years ago he got very angry with me. . . . He asked for a special painting that Mrs. Cleets had done years before. I looked for it, but it had disappeared."

"Do you know what happened to it?" Ma asked.

"Not long before that, I was out gathering fruit when someone entered the mansion and took some things." There was a long pause. "Several valuable things were missing. But it's odd that I didn't notice the painting missing right away . . . not until I searched did I realize it was gone." Sulia sighed heavily. "It must have been stolen at the same time and I just didn't notice it."

"I'm sorry," Ma said. "But it wasn't your fault that the painting was missing. . . ."

"No." Sulia's voice was almost a whisper now.

Abby sat up straight. "No, but Kaliman didn't believe me. He thought I was just keeping it from him. That's what hurt the most." Then Sulia began to cry. Hearing her mother begin to comfort Sulia, Abby quietly got up and left.

She climbed the stairs and joined Sarah in their dimly lit room. "Keep the light on, Abby," Sarah pleaded.

"All right," she said, noting her sister's frightened face. Abby changed into her nightdress. "But, Sarah, we're safe here." It was just as well, she thought as she slid between the sheets, because she was curious about the letters in Mrs. Cleets's box. Abby prayed for Sarah, and her sister soon turned away from the lit candle. Her breathing sounded deep and regular in no time.

Abby retrieved the letters from her bedside and sifted through them. But no sooner had she opened the first yellowed sheet than she heard Uncle Samuel and Lani speaking from the back porch. The sound of their voices rose up to her window, and Abby's interest picked up when she heard the word *dragon.*

"Samuel, if the beasts get as large as Abby said, don't you think they'd be slow moving?" Lani asked.

"Unfortunately, lizards are quick. I went down to check the prints before nightfall, and I'm afraid that's what we've got here. A giant lizard. By the depth of the paw prints and tail print, I can tell this was a 200- to 300-pound beast. A true dragon in our modern era. Perhaps a living dinosaur! I don't believe Western science even knows of it yet. It's incredible, and I hope to see it before we leave the island. I have no doubt it moves very quickly, at least for short distances. Much like the alligators in the southern swamps of America."

The back screen door creaked open and slapped shut. Abby made out Ma's voice as she joined them in a late-night talk. "I heard that, Samuel. Now I'm truly worried about the children. I'm ready to leave this island and get away from the danger, but I hate to leave dear Sulia here alone. I wish there was some way to solve her dilemma before we sail away."

Uncle Samuel sighed heavily. "The creatures probably avoid humans, Charlotte, as most wild animals do. . . ."

The talking continued, but Abby no longer listened. She started reading the letter and instantly became engrossed in the message that was addressed to Mrs. Cleets's sister, who lived in York-shire, England. Abby wondered why the letter had never been sent as she scanned the first few para-graphs, which were an outpouring of her grief over the death of her husband.

As the letter continued, Mrs. Cleets confided in her sister. "We aren't really sure what happened to Charles, as we only found his gun and hat near the path he took to the hunting grounds."

As Abby read the next few words, her heart picked up speed. A frightening story was unfolding before her eyes—a story that gripped her until the last word was read.

Chapter Eleven

When Abby read the word *dragons* in Mrs. Cleets
letter, she sat engrossed:

> *The islanders have told me they have seen these*
> *huge beasts waiting beside deer trails, hidden in*
> *brush and camouflaged for hours. Their yellow*
> *tongues flick in and out, tasting the air for*
> *nearby prey. Then they lunge! Nothing can*
> *escape, I'm told. They are too quick, too vicious,*
> *too strong.*
>
> *Charles says the beasts are "stealth preda-*
> *tors," but I call them dragons. I've heard rumors*
> *that they eat their own young when they are first*
> *hatched if the small lizards do not scurry into*
> *the nearest tree. Alas, if only they would stay in*
> *the trees and never descend! But they do, dear*
> *sister, and I fear my Charles has paid the ulti-*
> *mate price for bringing these creatures to our*
> *once-peaceful island. As I have written before,*
> *Charles brought several different creatures from*
> *other islands to our home here. The mouse deer,*

the civet, and even the babirusa pig that he captured on other islands.

How I begged him not to loose the ferocious dragons upon our happy paradise. But he would not listen to me. "We must have a predator to control the large deer population," he said. The deer, you see, were eating too many of our nutmegs. But this time Charles was wrong. The consequences have cost far too much. The islanders have never been happy about the dragons, and now there is unrest on the planta-tion with Mr. Cleets's disappearance. Many parents fear for the lives of their children, I'm told.

I will send this on with the next ship that stops for trade and is heading your way, unless by some lucky chance a British ship puts in and they are willing to take me to England with them. That's right, dear Annabelle, I am return-ing home as soon as I can. I intend to leave this all behind. My heart cannot bear to live here without Charles, and so you may see me sooner than you expected. I long for your company now—and for family and home.

Your loving sister,
Gwenyth

Abby's palms grew slick as she read the distress-ing news. Sarah was right after all! The dragons did eat people—one probably ate Mr. Cleets! She set the letter back in the box and leaned over to blow out the candle. All was quiet now. Everyone had gone to bed. Abby lay back on her pillow and closed her eyes. Mrs. Cleets must have sailed away on the very next ship that came in, leaving her unhappy memories and letters behind. But she also left Paloa and Sulia's village to live with the dangerous dragons that her husband had brought to this island.

Unsettled, Abby tossed and turned, trying to get comfortable in bed. Images of the giant dragon kept flashing through her mind.

Think pleasant, happy thoughts, she told herself. But that giant hulking dragon filled her head. She could see it turn her way. Its thick lizard head and powerful neck—with an eye that looked almost intelligent. It knew how to hunt! *It would eat me if it could!*

Abby remembered Sarah's bloodcurdling scream, and a prickling sensation raced up her neck.

This can't be happening. Maybe Mr. Cleets wasn't killed by a dragon. Maybe there's some other explanation. But as she inched closer to Sarah for comfort, she couldn't imagine what that other reason could be.

"Aaaahhh!"

Abby bolted up in bed only two hours after she'd finally fallen asleep. Sarah was sitting up in the dark next to her, screaming loud enough to wake the bats in the warehouse. "What's wrong?" Abby said, becoming fearful herself because Sarah was so convincing.

Ma arrived in the room carrying a lit candle. She set it down quickly and gathered a terrified Sarah into her arms. "What is it, darling?"

"The monster almost got me, Ma," Sarah said, gasping for breath. "It chased me and almost ate me!"

"No," Ma said soothingly, "it can't get you, and it wouldn't want to eat you. . . ."

Abby almost corrected Ma but realized this wasn't the time to mention Mr. Cleets's disappearance. She was beginning to feel the same fear with which Sarah was obsessed.

"Don't go, Ma," Sarah said, gripping Ma's arm tightly.

"Maybe you better come to bed with me, honey, and let Abby get some sleep." Sarah got out of bed, and the two left with the candle.

Abby lay back down with a sigh. Now it seemed that the dark, scaled dragon moved in the shadows of her room. Fear made her lie in bed uneasily, alert to every sound. She didn't want to be shut up in this room all alone. Abby rose and opened the bedroom door so Ma could hear her if she screamed.

A moment later she heard Pa's voice. "Sleep on the bench downstairs? It's a mess, Charlotte. . . ." Apparently, there wasn't enough room for three in

her parents' bed. "And there's a monkey down
there—" She heard Pa snort in frustration, but then
his footfalls started down the stairs.

It certainly wasn't fair that a horrible lizard was
ruining everyone's lives. Anger welled up inside
Abby. Why had God allowed it? Why did they have
to land at *this* island? It was full of danger! First
earthquakes and now man-eating dragons!

"It's not fair," she whispered angrily, punching
her pillow to make it more comfortable. "Isn't it
enough that we had to fight off pirates in the China
Sea?" Her mind traveled back to the day the pirates
had boarded their sleeping ship—and the moment
the pirate king had pressed his gleaming dagger
against Ma's soft white throat. Abby would never
forget the look in Ma's frightened eyes. Her pulse
quickened thinking about it.

She yanked the sheet up to her neck. Now they
were in danger again. Actually, *she* was in danger
more than anyone. If she encountered a dragon,
she'd never be able to outrun it, and she often
needed help getting up in trees. So why had God
given her weak legs? Why couldn't she have been
born "normal," like Sarah and Luke and all the
other kids she knew? Having weak legs couldn't be
God's best for her, could it? It *had* to be a mistake,
or maybe . . . maybe God just didn't love her as
much as others.

*I know You're in charge of everything, God, that
You can do anything You please. So why didn't it*

please You to give me normal legs? This question echoed in Abby's mind for a long time, haunting her.

The wind whispered through her open window, carrying the ripe scents of nutmeg fruit and frangipani. The forest sounds were muted at this late hour. All was calm. But there was no peace in Abby's heart as she tried to go back to sleep. If her reasoning was correct, it meant that either God wasn't really in control of everything, because having weak legs had to be a mistake . . . or it meant He wasn't fair.

Or could it be that He didn't love her as much as the others? Which was it?

Chapter Twelve

Abby groaned in frustration when the "wake up" bird screeched. She was tired and grumpy. After a breakfast of warm cassaba melon, "sweet as sugar candy," Luke said, they listened to Pa give orders.

"No wandering off by yourself alone," he commanded. "And your mother doesn't want you out hiking unless Paloa takes you on trails that she knows are completely safe and well traveled, understood?"

"Yes, Pa," Abby said. Luke looked depressed by the new rules, which he apparently didn't think were necessary.

"You don't have to worry about me," Sarah piped up. "I'm not leaving the mansion without Ma."

Soon Paloa showed up with Timor in tow, and Sarah thanked her. "What for?" Paloa asked.

"For bringing Timor. He's going to have a tea party with me, Sandy, Mr. Looloo, and Snuffles the pig. Do you think they'll like cinnamon tarts?" Sarah asked.

"I know Timor and Mr. Looloo will love them,"

Paloa assured her, "and I've never seen Snuffles turn down *any* food."

"Ah," Duncan teased, "then Snuffles and Luke have a lot in common." He reached out and ruffled Luke's blond-streaked hair. The two began to tussle and wrestle until Ma ordered them out onto the back veranda.

With all the jovial talking, Abby felt foolish about her nighttime fears. "Let's go exploring," she encouraged Paloa, "on safe paths, of course."

"We'll join you," said Uncle Samuel. Lani gave them a lovely smile, her aquamarine eyes shining with happiness.

With Sarah and the animals occupied, the troop set out along a familiar path they'd all traveled before. Paloa and Luke led the way.

Uncle Samuel taught them about lianas, the many different vines growing down from the forest canopy. A few flowered, revealing fragrant, appealing blossoms that were frequented by all types of insects. Abby had brought her journal and pencils, and she drew sketches throughout the hike of the various lianas. "Some of these are three or four inches thick," she said to Uncle Samuel.

"Good observation," he said. "One that thick could almost be used as a rope."

They encountered a great bird with a giant beak that Uncle Samuel called a "hornbill," colorful ground pheasants, and brush turkeys.

Luke sighted a tree snake with colorful markings that actually matched the flower blossoms of the branch on which it rested. It blended in perfectly and would have gone unnoticed but for its movements.

Frogs, geckos, skinks, and rats raced for cover as they passed. Among the ground animals was a wild pig that snorted a warning at them. "It's the *babi-rusa*," Paloa said. "Stay back—they can be aggressive."

Uncle Samuel herded them to the other side of a banyan tree to hide as they watched the pig trot off.

"Did you see its tusks?" Luke said, whistling. "They're growing right through the roof of its mouth."

The longer they stayed in hiding, the more wildlife they saw. Paloa eagerly pointed out a buck with antlers, his doe nearby. But when the frightened deer saw them, they made a wild barking sound as they leapt away. "They are called *barking deer*," Paloa explained. "They make that bark when they are scared."

"They sound like Sandy, don't they?" Abby said with a giggle.

On the way home, they saw two miniature island deer, no more than 14 inches tall, scampering about in the brush. Abby and Luke stood openmouthed in amazement.

"Those are mouse deer," Paloa explained. "They are called *pelanduk*. And they are beloved in these islands as folk heroes. Many stories tell how the *pelanduk* outwit their enemies with cleverness since they are too small to win with strength."

"The deer almost look magical," Abby said, enchanted. "Like something from a fairy tale. Did you see their delicate little hooves?"

"I admit they are cute," Luke said. "I'm going to call you *Pelanduk* from now on, Abby."

She looked at him curiously. "Why?"

"Well, you might not have the strength of some people, but you have a habit of outwitting your enemies, too."

Abby laughed. "I'll take that as a compliment. But this is definitely a strange island," she said, taking notes for her required composition. She began to wonder if they'd see a mythical unicorn in this fairy-tale forest where plants grew down from the sky and banyan tree roots grew up out of the ground.

On this remote island, she reflected, some deer barked like dogs, other tiny ones outwitted enemies, and dragons still roamed.

But as they headed back toward the mansion late in the afternoon, they saw no mythical creatures— dragons or otherwise.

That night, Abby and Sarah worked on the story they would tell using the *wayang* puppets. Since they had some characters that couldn't be represented by Sulia's puppets, Abby and Sarah cut out two-dimensional shapes from banana leaves and paper and tied them to bamboo sticks to add to the cast of characters they had planned. So when they had finally cleaned up their mess, Abby was tired.

"I'm sleeping with Ma again," Sarah told Abby, as she retrieved her nightdress from their room.

"Sarah, you know that God keeps you safe. Why don't you come back to bed and let Pa sleep with Ma? He's not too happy sharing that old couch with Mr. Looloo."

"I know God keeps me safe, Abby. But sometimes it's nice to have a real body in bed next to you. . . ."

"Well, what about me?" Abby asked.

"It's not the same as having Ma beside me," Sarah answered.

"Remember that Bible verse we memorized last year? 'I will lie down and sleep in peace, for You alone, O Lord, make me dwell in safety,' " Abby said.

"I'll keep it in mind," Sarah said, scampering off to Ma's bed.

"Sugar lumps," Abby complained, crawling between the sheets. Although she was tired of having to share a bed with Sarah, it had bothered her a lot less since the dragon incident. Now she laid her head on the cool pillow and thought she'd be asleep in minutes. Her legs were so tired from the long hike.

Relaxing in the quiet, Abby began to drift off when the candle on her nightstand began rattling. A rumbling noise outside startled and woke her. The candle crashed onto the floor and the bed began to tremble and move. She bolted up and threw off the sheet.

"Maaa!" she heard Sarah squeal.

By the time Abby had raced out of her room and into the hall, the swaying motion of the floor had ceased. But the pounding in her heart had not.

She heard Ma calming Sarah in her parents' bedroom. Luke, too, had woken up and rushed into the hall. He stood grinning at her, Sandy at his heels. "Just another little earthquake," he said sleepily, rubbing his tousled, sun-bleached hair. "Go back to sleep." He headed through his doorway with Sandy trotting after him.

"You're right," she said, trying to sound light-hearted. But as she headed to her own room, she realized that, for just a second, she'd thought it was a dragon pounding up the stairs.

She lay alone in bed for a long time, trying to concentrate on peaceful thoughts. Abby remembered what she'd told Sarah. *You alone, O Lord, make me dwell in safety.* She knew it was true, but sometimes it was hard to believe that . . . especially in the dark night when earthquakes rumbled the very bed you slept in. *Why are there so many earthquakes on this little island?* she wondered.

For the second night in a row, she punched her

pillow and heaved a sigh. Luke had Sandy to cuddle, and Paloa had Timor to sleep with. *But I get Sarah, who's mostly a bother,* she thought grumpily. *And not even here when I need her!*

Abby and Sarah spent the next morning working out the puppet show they would give that night after an early supper. By lunchtime, Paloa had arrived, bringing fresh fish for the evening meal. The girls spent time up in Abby's room talking during an afternoon thunderstorm. Luke joined them an hour later. Another piece of the Kaliman puzzle fell into place for Abby when she said to Paloa, "Tell me about your mother."

"I never knew her, of course. But Father has told me a little about her. She was kind and generous of spirit, he says. But it is hard for him to speak of her. She died right after I was born, and I don't think he's ever gotten over it." Paloa pushed her long dark hair off her shoulder and sighed.

"When Mother died, Father grew very angry. I think he blamed himself because he said to me, 'If I had offered tribute to the fertility god, then she would not have died.' He blamed Grandmother also, because she had convinced him to quit offering gifts to idols."

Abby sighed. "How awful for Sulia."

"Yes. And then Mr. Cleets died, too! That was the last straw for Father. He convinced his friends on the plantation that they should return to the old ways. He said if there is only one true God, that God should have protected Mr. Cleets—because Mrs. Cleets believed in Him. So there must not be just one god. He led the people back to the village and the old ways."

"What are the old ways?" Abby asked.

"Now my father tries to please many gods. . . . He gives gifts and offerings, and he wants me to also."

"What do you mean?" Luke asked as he took out a rope to practice knot tying.

"Father is especially afraid of the volcano," Paloa said. "He thinks we must honor the volcano god so it won't erupt. The people believe there are gods for every part of nature—you know, there are gods of trees, of rocks."

"Are there gods of the ocean and lakes?" Abby asked.

"The people think the ocean and waters are inhabited by demons," Paloa explained. "So they give a tribute to them to keep them happy."

Abby shook her head at this news. *How sad!*

"So," Paloa continued, "if my people want a big harvest, they give gifts. Or they leave out gifts so they won't be cursed with illness and death."

"It sounds like the people live in fear," Luke said.

Paloa nodded sadly. "Yes, my father is afraid. He

doesn't want me to die, so he does everything to please the gods. I have seen him kill our chickens and leave them on banana leaves in the forest as special offerings. I don't like it when he does that."

"And that's why Sulia won't go back to live in the village?" Abby asked.

"Yes." Paloa watched Luke toying with the rope, her face a mask of hopelessness. "I don't know what can untangle the knot of anger inside my father."

Abby gazed into Paloa's dark chocolate eyes. "And you are caught between the two. . . ."

Paloa nodded, biting her lower lip and wiping away a tear. An instant later Paloa hurried from the room. Abby heard her pounding down the stairs and rushing out the back door.

Abby's heart went out to her. *Poor, poor Paloa!*

Chapter Thirteen

When the sun broke through again and the jungle sounds revived, Abby and Luke went down to find Paloa. She was sipping sweet hibiscus tea and munching a cinnamon roll Sarah and Ma had made the day before. "These are good," she said, apparently cheered up again.

Luke grabbed one off the plate and joined her at the veranda table. "What do your people think of these earthquakes?" he asked.

"Oh, they're frightened that the earth god is unhappy about something. I would not be surprised if Father and his friends have sacrificed a chicken to appease the earth god."

"Let's go see if they did!" Luke said. "It'll be fun to get out of the house, anyway. The air is clean and fresh, and I need to stretch my legs."

"All right," Paloa said slowly. "But I hope I'm wrong."

"Me, too," Abby agreed. "But it'll be fun to see the butterfly glade again, anyway."

Abby's words seemed to encourage the young girl. "I have a good place to show you. It is a special place where the mouse deer, the *pelanduk,* live." Her brown eyes danced with such eagerness that Abby wanted to see it, too.

Soon the three were heading along the jungle path in the green twilight.

"I know a little shortcut," Paloa said, as she led them off the beaten track they'd traveled before. "It will save us 15 minutes of hiking."

Abby was all for saving steps. She'd had to rest twice already, and she was a little embarrassed to be slowing them down. "Is it safe, though?" she questioned, remembering Pa's stern warning.

"I have taken it several times," Paloa said.

"It's safe," Luke said, his mind evidently made up. "Let's go."

The forest floor was fairly clear. Only large ferns and huge tree trunks barred their way, with the many liana vines descending from the upper branches. It was easy to navigate until they came upon a spot where two large banyans had fallen some time back, opening the tree canopy above. Normally, direct sunlight never hit the forest floor. Shafts of rare sunlight now reached the forest floor in this area, and the plants had taken advantage of it.

A riot of growth had shot up: huge ferns, young trees, and bushes. Abby and Luke followed Paloa slowly through it. Just as they got into the shaded canopy again, an unusual profusion of vines hung down. Abby busily swatted them out of the way as she tried to hurry and keep up with Luke and Paloa. Then her foot slid forward in a depression still filled with yesterday's rain. Abby lost her footing on the slippery mud. She careened forward, slid downward, and kept going—down, down, down along a muddy chute. She landed with a loud *thud* at the bottom of a shallow cave.

"Hey!" she called, looking back up and seeing a bit of blue sky in the distance. "I'm stuck down here!" Her ankle instantly began hurting. She'd twisted it in the fall, and it was bent under her still. She moved so that she was lying on her tummy, peering toward the opening at a 30-degree angle.

I can claw my way back up, she thought. But as she tried, the slippery mud wouldn't give her a hold. It was too wet. The walls of the denlike tunnel were saturated with mud. Abby could make out grooves and cuts in the walls, and she wondered about them. In fact, now that she took a moment to assess her surroundings, she wondered how a tunnel had gotten here. She'd seen no other tunnels in the forest.

And what is that horrible stench? She turned to peer into the dark recesses by her feet, to see if the tunnel went on behind her. But no, it was pitch-black that way. Besides, something lay in the way. It looked like rocks piled up in a uniform way. *How odd!* She bent down in the cramped space and put her hand out.

She touched a smooth round surface and pulled it through the mud toward her. Luke and Paloa called her name. "Here!" she cried out as she brought the interesting stone toward her. Under the crust of mud the stone looked creamy white. And egg shaped.

Abby's heart skipped a beat. It *was* an egg! A clutch of giant, rock-hard eggs.

As if it burned her hand, she hastily pushed it back where she'd found it. Peering toward the light at the top of the tunnel, Abby saw again the deep scratch marks in the walls. Scratch marks like the ones she'd seen on that tree trunk where the deer meat had been hanging. With a sickening wrench of her stomach, she suddenly realized what had stolen the hanging meat from the tree. And she now knew what had caused those ferns to move and make her feel as if she were being hunted. She realized exactly where she was.

She'd fallen into the den of a dragon—a mother dragon!

"Luke!" she screamed. "Get me out of here!"

Chapter Fourteen

Luke turned back at the sound of Abby's muffled voice. Thick vines hanging from the branches above brushed his face. He moved them aside to see better.

"Abby?" he called. She'd been right behind him, but now she was out of sight. "Wait up, Paloa!" he yelled out. "Let's not get separated. Abby's disappeared."

Paloa's long silky hair swung as she pivoted and hurried back, a slight scowl on her tanned face. "Disappeared? You mean Abby's gone?"

"No, she wouldn't leave us," Luke said. "But she's missing. Come on, let's retrace our steps."

They'd no sooner reached the break in the overhead canopy when they heard Abby's scream. Luke's green eyes registered surprise—especially since the scream came from the ground.

He hurried toward the sound, scanning the earth for tracks. "Where are you?" he yelled.

"Down here, in a muddy—" Luke heard the panic in Abby's voice now—"dragon's den!"

Luke thrust aside a fern and kneeled where the ground showed a small stone outcropping. It sloped away into a cave. "How on earth," he muttered as Paloa joined him and poked her head down into the hole.

She quickly yanked her head out. "Eww, that stinks bad! Dragons have very bad breath."

Luke stuck his head in the hole and pulled it out with a grimace of disgust.

"Abby, I don't believe in dragons," Luke teased with a chuckle, "but this den does smell like it's full of dragon dung. Present company excluded, of course."

But when he looked over at Paloa, she wasn't laughing. "It does smell like the dragons, Luke."

"There are eggs down here!" Abby shouted. "Get me out before their mother returns!"

"Abby, can't you crawl up?" Paloa asked as she leaned back into the dark hole with her nose pinched shut. Luke peered over her shoulder but couldn't see much in the darkness. The ground sloped away at an angle.

Abby's reply came out a bit muffled. "I've tried, but it's too slick and muddy. I-I don't have the strength."

Luke frowned. "This isn't funny. We should always carry a rope for this kind of possibility. But we don't have one . . . ," he rambled, "and we can't just leave Abby here while we go hunting for one because—"

But he didn't finish the sentence. Paloa had gripped his arm in a death hold. "What's that sound?" she whispered in a panic.

For a moment all Luke could think was, *What sound?* For suddenly the constant bird chatter and frog *re-deeps* had ceased. An eerie silence descended over the forest. Then he, too, heard it.

Heavy footfalls were coming closer. Luke's heart skipped a beat as he turned toward the noise and jumped to his feet—just in time to see a nine-foot dragon break into the clearing, perhaps 40 feet away. Her thick neck and flat head turned in one direction, then another, as her tongue waved in the humid air. It was so long that Luke wondered if she'd swallowed a yellow snake and it was trying to escape.

But her forward movement stopped all speculation as she broke down shrubs, ferns, and azaleas and lumbered toward them.

"Jehoshaphat!" Luke's mouth went dry as he watched the husky lizard come closer. Her yellow tongue flicked in and out, rapidly testing the air, and her head turned from side to side, as if she were honing in on the intruders. Paloa stepped backward and fell over a root. Luke stepped backward and fell over her.

As they scrambled up, Paloa's eyes raked the surrounding area for help. "We can climb the trees, but Abby will be kil—"

"No!" Luke shouted, and for an instant the

dragon paused, assessing the new sound and smell of humans. Her tongue soared a foot above her head to taste the scent of fear on the breeze. Luckily they weren't downwind, but upwind. But the beast still came steadily on.

Pulling out his pocketknife, Luke flipped it open and held its four-inch blade toward the dragon.

Paloa looked as if she couldn't believe he'd even bother with it. "That's not as long as an *ora*'s claws!" she shrieked.

But Luke didn't take time to answer. He desperately searched for a branch or anything with which to beat the creature back—back away from Abby!

"Luke!" Abby's muffled scream rose up, unnerving him. He had to keep the beast from her den, but he had a sinking feeling he was no match for her massive strength. She looked powerful—and as vicious as a wolverine. Already within 25 feet of them, Luke had to find a way to stop her. "God," he whispered, "help us!"

"Lianas!" Paloa said in a rush. "The vines!" As she glanced toward a nearby liana hanging down, Luke instantly understood.

He grabbed Paloa by the hand and yanked her to the foot of the liana-draped tree. Lifting her without warning, he boosted her to the first branch. "Here," he said, thrusting the knife handle at her, "cut one as high up as you can."

Paloa nimbly climbed higher, keeping one eye on the *ora* as she hurried. Twenty feet above the ground, she sliced through a three-inch thick liana and let it drop at Luke's feet. "Good," he yelled. "Abby, take the vine and wrap it around your middle." He tossed one end into the tunnel, holding the other. "Mama's home. There's no time to lose!"

A hiss filled the air. A low growl came from her massive throat and neck. The dragon pounded closer, within 10 feet now, and the ground vibrated with her coming.

"Luke, I can feel it!" Abby screamed. He swallowed hard. He'd never heard her sound so scared before—not even when they'd faced pirates, storms, or sharks.

And he had no choice but to leave her in the dragon's den while he climbed a tree.

Chapter Fifteen

Shooting into the tree that stood closest to the den, Luke took one end of the liana with him. He stood on an overhanging branch near the trunk and leaned out. The dragon was just feet from her den! Luke could hardly bear it. *Even if the vine holds and I pull Abby from the den—she's bound to meet that beast on her way out.*

God—we need help!

The dragon's head came up, and her tongue licked the sky as she tried to hone in on Luke.

"I've got it!" Abby yelled. "Pull!"

Will the vine hold her weight? Bracing his chest on another branch and one foot against a limb, Luke began to pull, hand over hand. The months of sailing and hauling rigging had built up his muscles, and he felt Abby's weight moving on the other end. Sweat glistened on his forehead as he strained to rescue her.

But the dragon was too close—almost at the den opening!

If she lunges at Abby when she comes up, Abby will be bitten and poisoned—or worse.

Luke closed his eyes as he heaved on the vine, focusing all his energy on hauling Abby up. Then, suddenly, he heard a loud growl. The earth trembled.

Another dragon, bigger and thicker, erupted into the clearing. It bore down on the first with a hissing screech like a boiling teakettle. Paloa screamed as the 12-foot lizard challenged the smaller female to the prey they both smelled. Luke chewed his lip in horror. The two dragons reared up on their hind legs, balancing on their tails. They could almost reach Luke and Paloa in their separate perches! Their dagger teeth showing, they tore at each other and crashed like titans into anything in their way.

The green vine was beginning to slip through Luke's sweating hands. He couldn't haul Abby up into the midst of that! But when the smaller of the two backed up, the giant one sprinted toward her.

Now!

Luke set into the vine like a madman, hauling as ferociously as the dragons fought. When he saw Abby's cinnamon hair break the top of the den, he redoubled his efforts.

Slick with mud, Abby emerged from the cave, clawing her way up as the vine hauled her heavenward. She struggled to stand, but Luke was pulling her so fast she was instantly lifted a foot above the ground. And for one brief second, she hung there, as the two titans crashed into each other, just six feet away! Rearing back on their thick tails, they

tore at each other's necks, too busy to notice Abby,
who was downwind. Long claws slashed into scaly
hide. They fell back to the ground and began to
circle—heading toward Abby. Their powerful tails
swayed like giant pythons, angling to hit one
another.

Luke yanked harder and Abby jerked upward.
Let the vine hold! he prayed.

Three feet, four, now six feet above the ground.
Abby swayed with each pull and grabbed the vine
above her in case the dragons lunged at her. Luke
knew she'd try to pull herself up out of harm's way.
But he also knew she didn't have much arm
strength. He hauled desperately, his own arms now
burning with the effort.

Now she was 10 feet above the ground, and both
her hands reached out to grip the tree limb on
which Luke stood. "Got it?" he panted.

When she nodded, he dropped the liana vine and
bent down to grab her wrist in one hand. Muscles
straining, he lifted her upward with one arm. She
clung to him as he steadied her on the branch.
When a small sob escaped her, he held her tight,
trying to calm her shaking.

"You're safe now," he said softly. Luke bit his lip.
That was close. Too close. She was still trembling, so
he moved her closer to the tree trunk, where she
could sit down and rest.

Below them the dragons hissed, surged at one
another, and reared again. Their deadly fight

showed exactly how much damage they could do. The smaller dragon was bleeding. When the big one whipped its tail and knocked the smaller one off her feet, she cowered in submission. The victor flicked its tongue, stretching its neck now toward the tree in which Abby and Luke sat. With the battle done, it looked back to its prey while the female dragged herself toward her den to hide and lick her wounds.

The big one neared the tree and began searching for the dinner that got away. Its tongue spat out, its beady eyes searched the limbs. Standing up on its hind legs, the dragon leaned against the trunk and stretched toward Abby. The tree trembled with its weight. Abby shrieked and almost fell off as she scrambled to stand up and climb higher.

"Be careful!" Luke said in a panic, climbing behind her. "If you fall . . ."

The beast licked the air just below their feet.

"It's climbing the tree!" Abby screeched.

"No, Abby," Paloa said from her tree nearby. "Only young ones climb. You are safe."

As if it had heard Paloa, the beast finally dropped back on all fours. It wandered near the trunk of Paloa's tree, and she scurried up to a higher branch. It reared again, searching with tongue and marble-black eyes, then finally fell back to earth with a ground-shaking *thud*. For a few minutes, it searched the area, then finally left.

Abby dried off her sweaty palms on her skirt. Luke helped her climb down to a lower branch to sit more comfortably. "Well," he said after a few minutes of rest, "you ready to head home?"

"No!" Abby's cornflower-blue eyes blazed. "I'm not going to make it easy for those monsters."

Luke glanced over at Paloa, who nodded in agreement. "We'll wait. Then we'll run home fast!" She held a finger to her lips, indicating that they should be quiet and let the dragon in her den forget they were there.

Luke knew Abby couldn't run quickly, so he settled back against the tree trunk, hoping the dragons would soon forget them. He bumped her shoulder once and could feel her tense muscles. *But she was right,* he thought. *There are real live dragons on this island.* He cleared his throat and looked at her sheepishly.

"*Here Be Dragons,*" Luke said quietly, "might be the understatement of the century."

Abby glanced over at him. For the first time in a long while, her face relaxed. "I was praying the whole time I was down in that dragon's den," she said. "But who could have guessed the answer to that prayer would be another dragon?"

Luke nodded. "The big dragon sidetracked the smaller one, and their fight lasted just long enough to get you out of the den." He closed his eyes, his face solemn. He could hear the birds beginning to chatter and twitter again, as if the forest breathed a sigh of relief, too. "Thank You, God," he whispered.

Abby's curls were mud-caked, her skirt and face

smeared with goo, but she smiled. "I guess you don't need to be wearing armor to rescue a damsel in distress. . . ."

"Or," Luke quipped, "a damsel in dirt."

Abby tweaked his freckled nose. "Thanks, Sir Luke of the Kitchen Table."

Chapter Sixteen

Another 20 minutes passed. During their time in the tree, a flying snake flew by Abby's head and a bright blue skink landed on her hand, then leapt off in fear. Abby began to squirm with impatience, wondering what other creatures might slither or fall onto her auburn curls before the day was over. "Let's go," she whispered softly, standing up to start the climb down.

But when a distant rumbling and shaking began, Abby's mind instantly assumed another dragon was near. She could barely grasp that they were now experiencing an earthquake, too! She grabbed the tree with white knuckles.

"Another dragon!" Paloa yelled, searching the area as she, too, held on to a branch.

"Earthquake!" Luke corrected as he climbed next to Abby. The ground trembled violently, limbs cracked and fell. The whole island seemed to rock with unleashed power. Abby held on as the ground shook and trees swung like clock pendulums. Overhead the forest canopy waved like sea swells.

Birds took to wing, flying off with alarm. Abby could hear the distant barks of frightened deer. Another deep rumbling sounded in the distance, striking terror in her heart. Even Luke's green eyes looked scared as a 75-foot tree crashed to the forest floor, shearing the limbs from other trees in its path.

The wild shaking energized the female dragon, who streaked from her lair like a lit rocket. In fact, so fast that Abby realized she'd never be able to outrun one. The dragon disappeared from sight.

Abby clung to the tree trunk until the shaking stopped.

"Luke, let's get home!" she begged, eager to make sure that Ma, Sarah, and the others were all right, too. Luke nodded once, his face as sober as she'd ever seen it. She glanced over to make sure Paloa had survived, but the Indonesian girl was already descending from her perch.

From the lowest branch, Luke jumped to the ground and helped Abby down. Paloa joined them, her eyes darting around warily. "We'll move fast," she urged.

Abby's heart fell. *I can't move fast, and now my ankle's hurt,* she thought. *Oh, why did God give me slow legs—and these trials?*

Luke gripped Abby's hand in his wide one. "We'll make it," he promised, setting off at a fast walk. Abby winced but kept quiet about the throbbing in her ankle.

They had to take the trail, passing through the bushes where the sky broke through the canopy opening. This was frightening, because a dragon could be hiding behind the shrubs and ferns. Thankfully, none were.

As they headed back through the canopy-covered forest, the ground cleared out. Only tall tree trunks and a dotting of ferns and azaleas covered the moist, leafy ground. "Dragons lie waiting behind bushes, then attack," Paloa said. "If we see one come, we'll climb a tree. Then we'll be safe."

This thought comforted Abby. She might not be able to outrun one, but she could climb a tree with Luke's help.

Luke tugged her at a fast clip along the path they'd taken. After a while, Abby's ankles began to feel numb, but she ignored them and leaned on Luke when she started to trip. The way home felt much longer than the way there.

As they finally emerged from the jungle into the grassy area around the mansion's lake, Abby heard Paloa gasp. "Look!"

There on the other side of the lake were two giant dragons, at least as big as the large one they'd seen in the forest. One was climbing from the water, the lake still rippling from its movements.

"Let's go!" Luke said, breaking into a sprint and yanking Abby alongside him. She breathed hard, praying she wouldn't fall as her ankle pained her. As they got closer to the mansion, Ma stepped out on the back porch, the screen door banging shut behind her. A towel in hand, she shaded her eyes and watched them run toward the back porch. Her head swiveled, and Abby could see by the look on her face that she'd seen the dragons, too.

Ma hurried toward them, and Abby—dirty, gasping, and exhausted—fell into her arms. Luke watched them embrace, then herded them inside. Paloa stood gazing out at the dragons while Abby and Luke sat at the small kitchen table. Already her ankle felt better as she drank the hibiscus tea Ma poured them.

"Abby," Ma said in amazement, "why are you filthy with mud, and . . . what is that horrible stench?"

Abby felt her cheeks flame under the dried mud. "It's dragon dung, Ma. I . . . fell in one of their dens, and I need a bath."

Ma stood speechless as Sulia entered the kitchen, her eyes instantly widening at Abby's appearance.

"The dragons are stirred up," Paloa said.

"Probably because of the earthquakes," Luke added.

Paloa's eyes met Sulia's. "I have never seen such big ones—and so close," she told her grandmother.

Ma's hand pressed to her heart. Abby knew she wanted more information about her escape, but the conversation was moving too quickly.

"And so many earthquakes," Sulia said softly. "What can it mean?"

As Sarah bounded down the stairs and entered the kitchen, Ma gently steered her to sit with her back to the kitchen door.

"Usually they stay hidden," Paloa continued, not aware that Ma was trying to keep the news about the dragons away from Sarah. But Abby knew Ma didn't want Sarah to see them.

"Who?" Sarah asked. "Who stays hidden?"

"The dragons," Paloa answered. "See?" She pointed out the door to the remaining dragon near the lakeshore. Everyone turned to see.

Sarah's blue eyes opened with alarm. "Ma!" Sarah clung to Ma's waist. "It's coming, Ma! We've got to leave."

"Shhh," Ma scolded. "It can't come in the house!" She brushed a hand against her temple. "I hope your father and Duncan are all right," she said to Abby. "Sarah, come rest with me upstairs. I have a roaring headache and need to lie down."

Sarah obediently followed Ma up the stairs, gazing over her shoulder at Abby and Luke. "Don't go swimming, Abby!" she said, fear evident on her face.

"Don't worry, Sarah. I'm not going to the lake," Abby promised, although she needed to wash—badly.

The fear Sarah was suffering made Abby angry enough to forget washing at the moment. How dare those beasts threaten their lives! *There are real live dragons in the world, and our family has managed to stop in one of the few places on earth where they roam!*

Now she had to worry about Pa and Duncan getting safely home—which made her angrier still. And where were Lani and Uncle Samuel, anyway?

Her eyes spit fire as she scanned the kitchen, looking for a weapon with which she could protect her family. But would anything frighten those vicious scale-hided beasts? When her gaze landed on the empty black pot on the stove, she impulsively grabbed it and stomped onto the porch. The last dragon was sunning itself by the lake.

Anger surged through Abby like a tsunami. She brought the heavy lid down on the pot, crashing and clanging the two pieces together. She knew the loud sound would carry down to the lake, which formed a sort of amphitheater. Abby stormed off the veranda and began walking in the dirt toward the distant dragon as she clanged and banged the metal. She heard the screen door *thwack* shut and recognized Luke's footfalls behind her while she kept her eye on her enemy.

The dragon shook its head. Even from this distance she saw the yellow forked tongue shoot out in alarm. It rose up on its thick bowed legs and scurried off into the brush. Luke put a hand on Abby's shoulder to stop her from going any farther. As he saw the dragon's tail disappear into the surrounding field of grass, he hooted with delight. "That's my spunky Abby!" he said, steering her back toward the porch and kitchen. "Now let's allow your ma to take a nap, all right?"

Before they got to the kitchen door, however, Sulia and Paloa joined them out back. Sulia's lips were pressed into a grimace as she stood quietly. In the distance Abby heard a soft drumming and wondered what it was.

When she turned to Sulia, a question on her face, Sulia nodded. "Those are the *gamelan* drums," Sulia explained. "The village is trying to appease the earth god with the sacred drums. They are afraid. They think the earthquakes prove he is angry with them."

"But there is no earth god," Paloa said, frowning.

"No, and their drums will not work to stop the earth from shaking," Sulia said. "Nor will it work on those," she said, pointing to where the dragons had just disappeared, "for they are not gods either . . . only hungry beasts."

Sulia shook her head, despair crossing her sweet, wrinkled face. "Oh, my son, my son. When will you see the truth?"

Luke put an arm around Sulia's thin shoulders. "A lot of people get deceived, Sulia. Once I worshiped gold instead of God. I thought it would bring me security—and I guess Kaliman thinks that making gifts to gods will bring him security. . . . I had to learn the hard way, but Abby was praying for me and God helped me see the truth. So why don't we pray for your son right now?"

Abby watched Sulia almost burst into tears at

Luke's kindness. But she got control of herself as they all filed into the kitchen and sat at the table. Reaching out to take her hand, Luke led them in prayer for Kaliman and for protection during any further earthquakes or dragon dangers.

After it was over, Luke got up and took the zinc washtub down from the kitchen wall. He set it down on the kitchen floor as he kneeled in front of Abby. "I beg you, O Queen of the Dragon's Den, to take a bath for the sake of your suffering subjects!"

Paloa giggled at Luke's words. "Abby, I have a much better idea. Instead of building up the fire, drawing water from the creek, and heating it up for a bath, let's go along the beach to my secret grotto. You can soak in the hot spring there! It's wonderful to sit in."

Abby bit her lip. "I don't want to run into any more dragons. . . ."

"I've never seen them on the beaches," Paloa said, "and we can get to the grotto from the beach—we'll take that short walk through the cave."

Abby remembered the beautiful grotto and thought of the pleasure of soaking in a bubbling warm bath. And they had left the torch outside the cave exit. It would be worth the walk, since her ankle was feeling better now. "Okay, I'll borrow some of Luke's Chinese matches."

Luke gladly gave them some matches. "If it will help you smell better," he teased. The girls punched him playfully and headed out, making good time along the beach. The walk through the tunnel was uneventful, and when they emerged they leaned the torch against a rock wall.

Abby went straight to the hot spring, took off her boots, and climbed in with all her clothes on. She sank down on a stone ledge next to Paloa and grinned as the bubbles lifted away the slimy mud from clothes and skin. "This is the easiest washing I've ever done."

Paloa grinned. "I want to show you something when we're done."

"I don't want to go into the jungle again," Abby cautioned.

"No, it's here in the cave."

Frangipani petals blew across the cavern floor on a warm wind. Abby lay her head back and scrubbed the caked mud from her curls. Twenty minutes later the girls emerged dripping but clean. Paloa promised that their uncomfortably wet clothes would dry in minutes as they sat in the late-afternoon sun on some boulders.

In five minutes they were dry enough to head into Paloa's shallow cave. She gently lifted the cloth-wrapped picture off the old sea trunk and set it aside. Then she raised the lid and dug through it. When she brought out a long, *batik*-patterned cloth of turquoise and one of crimson, Abby's eyes brightened. "Oh, those are beautiful!"

"They're silk scarves," Paloa said, holding up the

crimson one to Abby. "Yes, this color will be beautiful with your eyes. The other one is for Sarah, to cheer her up after all her fear." Paloa began to tie the long scarf around Abby's waist. She knotted it efficiently over Abby's denim waistband and smiled as the scarf ends hung down. "You look pretty."

Abby twirled happily, then threw her arms around Paloa. "Thank you. I love it! And I know Sarah will be thrilled, too."

"Good." Paloa put the trunk lid down. Almost reverently, she replaced the wrapped picture on it. "Let's get to the mansion now. Dinner might be ready."

Chapter Seventeen

Over a scrumptious meal of skewered fish and spiced rice, the dinner conversation turned toward the dangerous dragons and frequent earthquakes.

"In Hawaii, many earthquakes often means the volcano is about to erupt," Lani said, her sky-blue eyes solemn.

Abby grew nervous at that thought.

Uncle Samuel laid a large hand over Lani's on the table. "I hope that's not the case here. In 1815 this part of the world had the biggest eruption known in the history of mankind. A place called Tambora. Over 80,000 people died from Tambora's eruption. So much ash was thrown into the sky that the sun was darkened for months on end. Crops couldn't grow, and it was called 'the year without summer.' Throughout the world, people starved and disease broke out."

Luke sat up straight. "That must have been one *big* lava flow."

"I've read about it," Uncle Samuel said. "Although there was lava, these Indonesian volcanoes erupt with more of an explosion than a lot of liquid. Rocks fly, gas and steam blows out, and ash makes it hard to breathe."

Sulia nodded. "I remember it well. Kaliman was still a small boy. It was cold and dark that year. Many people died from the *lahars*."

"What's a *lahar?*" Abby asked.

"It's a mudflow—when the rocks and ash mix with a river up high on the mountain, it turns into a river of mud pouring down the mountainside."

"It moves very fast," Uncle Samuel agreed, "and picks up trees and objects in its way, which makes it even more deadly."

"Lovely," Luke said, recalling that several streams ran down Mount Bakat.

Pa glanced at Sarah, then set his napkin on the table and stood up. "Why don't we put our minds on other subjects now? Didn't we have a puppet show scheduled?"

Abby's mind instantly switched gears as she and Sarah jumped up and disappeared into the sitting room while the others cleared dishes. Pa's words meant it was time for their version of a shadow puppet show.

After the meal, Luke and Paloa gathered the goat, Sandy, Mr. Looloo the ape, and Nutmeg the parrot all around them in the sitting room. Ma, Pa, Uncle Samuel, Lani, Sulia, and Duncan sat around the room on the bench and two chairs. They all stared expectantly at the white sheet, now lit up by two lanterns and three candles. When Timor tried to nibble the sheet, Paloa scolded him and held on to his collar.

Luke tried not to smile, but he could hear Abby whispering fierce instructions to Sarah. "Don't forget to do what I told you!" Her voice carried beyond the sheet, telling Luke she was a tad nervous about tonight's performance.

A short drumroll on a tin can by Sarah, who wielded two pencils as drumsticks, alerted everyone that the show was about to begin. Bells tinkled, and Abby cleared her throat. "Tonight's performance comes from Scottish folklore."

"Snord the Ferocious," she began as Sarah worked the dragon puppet, "was a menace to the good people of the highlands. . . ."

The dragon soared overhead, making angry growls. Sarah's voice, lowered to sound mean, said, "I'm hungry! I think it's time to eat some sheep."

Soon Stuart and Curly the sheep were introduced and Stuart's hopeless problem explained. "But," Abby the narrator said, "Stuart prayed and God gave him a dream. If he would have courage to risk his life, he had a chance to rescue his best friend!"

Abby worked the Stuart puppet, showing him stirring a pot of cake batter. Sarah held up the silhouette of several large cakes. "No one had ever fed a dragon rice before. But it was a good idea because dragons' bellies are full of fire! And when Snord ate the uncooked rice, it quickly began puffing up in his stomach."

As the ferocious Snord began to eat the cakes with the rice hidden inside, Sarah held the dragon puppet while Abby held a pig bladder over his stomach. Then she blew into the bladder, making it blow up and up and up like an expanding stomach.

Chuckles erupted from the audience, and Sarah's eyes glowed with delight at the response.

When Stuart saved the sheep and led them home, everyone applauded. Abby and Sarah, both in their new scarves, emerged from behind the sheet to take their bows.

Longhaired Lani gave Abby a knowing look. "I think the stage beckons, Miss Kendall. You have talents we didn't know about." She patted Abby's cheek. "Do it again soon."

Sulia gave both Abby and Sarah hugs and spoke in her singsong voice. "I enjoyed hearing a new tale—and one with our God in it."

Paloa pushed her long silky hair off her shoulder and grabbed Abby's hand. "I have never heard that story, Abby. Is it true?"

Abby's eyes twinkled with mystery. "You'll have to ask Duncan—the resident Scotsman of our clan."

Ma reached out and squeezed Abby's shoulder.

"Good job, honey. And thank you for having Sarah work the dragon puppet. I think it helped her feel more in control of our situation here."

Abby nodded. "I hope Sarah will sleep better now."

As Pa and Duncan grabbed their rifles to walk Paloa home, Abby hugged her friend good-night. "See you tomorrow."

"Can we plan a puppet show for tomorrow night?" Paloa asked eagerly.

Abby nodded and grabbed Luke by his sleeve. "And we'll get Luke to help us."

"I'm not going to help with any old puppet show," Luke began to mumble.

Abby rolled her eyes and walked Paloa out to the waiting adults. Lani and Samuel wanted to go with them in the bright moonlight. Abby watched them leave. When Paloa reached the footbridge, she turned and lifted her hand. Paloa smiled and began to walk toward the village. It was good to see Paloa happy, Abby thought.

The moon was so bright that Abby wished for curtains. She tossed and turned, listening to distant sounds of crickets and frogs. An hour had passed, but her mind wouldn't settle down and let her tired body rest.

A spice-scented breeze blew through the window,

but the beauty of the island seemed false to Abby now. Especially after the day she'd had.

Yes, that dinner conversation had made her realize even more that this island had a dark side. "Take your pick," she whispered to the dark, "death by dragons or exploding volcanoes."

Her terrifying moments in the dragon's den flooded her mind. She'd felt so trapped and helpless—and slow when she'd tried to run back to the mansion.

Now her throat grew dry, her muscles tense. If God knew she was going to need to escape dangers, why had He given her such slow legs? *I just want to be normal, God.*

The moonlight was as bright as day. Abby climbed out of bed and headed down the hall toward the stairs. She could hear Ma's and Sarah's regular breathing as she passed their room. Down she wandered, toward the kitchen. *I'll pump some water and have a drink. Maybe then I'll be able to go to sleep.*

But when she got to the kitchen, she was surprised to see Pa sitting out under the stars on the back porch. He seemed to be gazing up at the diamond points.

She softly opened the back screen door and joined him. "Hi, Pa. What are you doing?" She sat down near him. His blond hair looked silver in the light.

"Aw, that monkey in there bothers me no end. I

think its fleas have bitten me, too. I'm itching some- thing fierce." He scratched the back of his neck.

Abby couldn't help smiling. "I'm sorry, Pa." She wanted to say more. She wanted to relieve the pres- sure in her heart, ask the questions going around in her head, but she held her tongue.

Yet Pa seemed to sense her mood.

"What's on your mind, Princess?" Pa reached out a thick hand in the moonlight. Abby took it and felt warmed.

"I can't keep up, Pa. Whenever we hike, I'm always the slowest." Pa listened quietly. Although he stared off into the stand of nutmeg trees, Abby knew he was listening to every word.

"And that doesn't seem fair, does it?"

"It's *not* fair. Why did God make me slow? I don't want to be different from other kids. And . . . and—" Abby groped for words—"if we're going to keep having adventures, why didn't He give me strong legs so . . ." Her heart churned with unspo- ken fear. "So I could outrun a dragon?"

Pa squeezed her hand and sighed. "Sometimes it's hard to see God's purpose ahead of time, Abby. But He always has one. I know it's not easy having slow legs, but God's given you other areas where you do better than some. You're quick-witted."

"I don't like being different, Pa. I want to be able to depend on my body the way Luke does. His body does whatever he needs it to."

Pa nodded and turned to gaze into her face. Abby saw love in his eyes.

"Sweetheart, maybe God doesn't want you to depend on your own strength. Maybe your weak legs are a gift—a gift because they remind you to depend on God more than on yourself."

"What do you mean, Pa?"

"Well, the truth is, it's foolish to depend on our own strength. We're all pretty puny compared to God." Pa scrubbed his cheek. "Do you remember David and Goliath, Abby?"

Abby nodded. "It's one of my favorite stories. But David was normal, Pa. He didn't have slow legs."

"True, but he sure couldn't equal the strength of the giant Goliath, could he? Goliath completely trusted in his big body and strength. But David, who was probably a young teen at that time, didn't trust in his skill or strength. He said, 'The battle is the Lord's.' The only thing he trusted in was God Almighty, and God won the victory for him."

Pa's hand wrapped around Abby's tightly. She could feel his calluses, his strength from years of work. "Are you saying that God's the One who makes things come out in the end? Is that what you mean?"

Thomas Kendall's smile lit up the dark night. "I'm proud of you, Daughter. I'm proud of your heart; I'm proud of your faith. I love the person you're growing into. Don't let yourself fall into that pit of self-pity over your weak legs. Sometimes the biggest danger we Christians face isn't a dragon, Princess. Sometimes the most deadly enemy comes so quietly we don't even notice it."

"What is it, Pa?"

"Discouragement—thinking that life is too difficult, that God's let it get too hard. That we don't deserve what we're getting. I've felt that way, so I understand how you're feeling. But usually we get to that point because somewhere along the line we've believed a lie about God. That He's not being fair or kind to us. That we deserve something better." Pa sighed. "Watch out, Abby. The enemy of our souls wants to trap us with that wrong thought."

Abby swallowed hard. He'd hit on her very problem. "How do you get out of that trap, Pa?"

Pa breathed in deeply. "God has a way to deliver us from that. Know what it's called? It's called the Trust-in-Him Highway. When I walk in faith on that high way, I always escape." He squeezed her hand affectionately. "God has great things in store for you, honey. But you won't get to enjoy them if you're stuck in self-pity."

Abby bit her lip. "I've already spent time there today—I definitely don't want to go back!" She gazed up at the glittering stars and sighed, feeling a new peace enter her. "I guess I need to accept myself the way God made me and find things to be grateful for."

Pa leaned over and kissed her cheek. "I'm thankful for you in my life, Princess. And I love the way God made you."

Pa's scent, like warm raisins, wood smoke, and wind reached Abby. Unlike Lani's plumeria blossoms, it was Pa's scent, she realized, that would always remind her of "home."

He had let her know that other people had these same thoughts and feelings. She wasn't the worst Christian in the world.

"Time to hit the bunk," Pa said. "I have a feeling sleep'll come easier now."

"Night, Pa," Abby said, rising and hugging his neck. "I love you."

Abby headed back upstairs and crawled into bed. As she plumped the pillow and laid down, she suddenly felt sleepy. She closed her eyes and began to drift to sleep while a melody rose to her window. Pa's voice, rich and sure, sang her a lullaby. Abby recognized the familiar hymn—"Amazing Grace."

> *Through many dangers, toils and snares*
> *I have already come;*
> *'Tis grace hath brought me safe thus far,*
> *And grace will lead me home.*

"Lord," Abby whispered, "I'm sorry for feeling sorry for myself . . . for not trusting You like I should. You *have* brought me through every danger so far, and You must have a good reason for making me different. Maybe just like Pa said—to help me trust in You and not in me. Please help me remember that it's okay to run slower and walk slower than others, as long as I'm walking in faith."

Chapter Eighteen

Breakfast had just finished around the dining-room table when Duncan tromped into the house from his morning walk to check on the ship. "A bonnie brig has just sailed into our bay!" he said excitedly. Pa and Uncle Samuel rose instantly to join him.

Ma took off her apron and smiled at Lani. "Maybe it's a family from Hawaii or California."

Lani, Sarah, and Luke jumped up from the table and headed toward the front door. "Sulia," Lani said, "join us. We're going to see who's come to call."

Sulia took off her apron, too, and hung it over a chair as Ma and the others headed out the door. Sandy the pup barked and raced after them, then plunged down the sand toward the shore.

Abby brushed her long curls off her shoulder. "Wait up! I want to come!"

Charlotte Kendall paused. "Abby, would you please be a dear and do the dishes quickly before you come down?"

Abby's face fell as she watched everyone leave and

head down the sandy path toward the anchored ship. But a few seconds later, Luke turned and frowned. She heard him sigh loudly and walk past the others back toward the house. When he returned to the front door, where she was standing, Abby grinned. "I love having a best friend," she said, handing him one of the women's aprons.

He chuckled, then surprised her by tying it on around his waist. Abby laughed as she gathered dirty dishes from the table and headed to the kitchen with them. "Hey," Luke suggested, "let's wash them out back in the zinc tub by the water pump." Luke would rather be outside any day.

He got the tub down and set the dishes in it. Together they carried it out to the back deck. "Nice idea," Abby admitted. "We can enjoy the day while we work and—hey, there's Paloa!"

Paloa was racing across the footbridge that spanned the distant creek. The look on her face and her dark hair streaming out behind her told Abby something was wrong.

Luke glanced up and set the dish he was holding back in the soapy tub. "Paloa," he hollered, waving a wet hand. Paloa's face didn't break into her typical smile. In fact, she looked as if she were about to burst into tears.

Luke and Abby hurried toward her. Paloa stopped and bent over. She was heaving from exertion, as though she'd run all the way from her village. Abby put a gentle hand on her back as the girl stood up and gasped for breath.

"Abby, Father has taken Timor to the sacrificial rock. He's going to sacrifice him to the volcano god!"

"No!" Abby exclaimed in shock. How could Paloa's father do that to her pet?

"Too many earthquakes," Paloa said, gasping. "Father says the gods are not pleased, and he will do anything to appease them!" She looked wild. "What should I do?"

Luke untied his apron and tossed it onto the porch. "How long ago did he leave?"

"He and six other men are heading there right now."

"Then we'd better go now if we want to rescue your goat," Luke said.

Paloa burst into sobs, and Abby gathered the petite girl in her arms. An instant later Paloa wiped her cheeks with a hand and sniffed. "Timor's pure brown coat makes him special. He is all brown like the earth, and that will make the earth god happy, Father said," she wailed. "My father believes the earth god controls the volcano."

Luke peered over Paloa's dark hair to Abby. "I'll be right back."

Abby pulled a cup from the soapy water and rinsed it, then gave Paloa a drink from the pump. As the winded girl drank, Abby thought how senseless it was. The earth was going to move, or erupt, no matter what Kaliman did or thought.

Seconds later Luke strode across the deck. He had a length of coiled rope slung over one shoulder and chest. "Let's go. Every second counts now if we want to save Timor."

Down the hill they hurried in the bright light of morning. Abby eyed the lake water, remembering the dragon as it climbed out after its swim and the rings that had shot out across the lake. Like those rings, the dragons' impact rippled across the whole island, changing everything. No one was safe from dragons or earthquakes here. *Although there are flowers and spice,* Abby couldn't help think, *not everything here is nice.*

As they entered the green twilight of the jungle, it was Paloa, who'd taken this trail many times, who led the way. It wasn't until that moment that Abby realized she hadn't told anyone where they were heading. If they hurried, and Ma found someone to talk to from the other ship, there was a slim chance they'd be able to return even before Ma did from the beach. Otherwise Ma would be worried.

They pressed on as fast as Abby could go. Although she grew tired quickly, she tried hard not to slow them down. She kept at it. The difference between life and death for sweet Timor might depend on how soon they got there.

They headed toward Bakat, the volcano, and the sacrificial rocks below it. The ground began to slope upward, and Abby pushed herself harder. Her legs felt like pudding, all wobbly and numb. She wanted to sit down. It had been 30 minutes of rapid hiking. When Luke stopped suddenly, she practically fell down. "Abby," he said, turning back to her, "do you need to rest?"

She swallowed. "Yes, but I think we have to keep going or we might not get there in time. Could I lean on your arm?"

"Of course," Luke said kindly as he held out his arm. "Let's go."

They pressed on, over sticks, through ferns, and up hilly mounds as they neared the foot of the mountain. The forest sounds were quiet but for insects and frogs—hundreds of them *re-deeping* in different pitches. Abby found it comforting. Perhaps if there were any dangers or dragons lurking behind ferns, the frogs would grow quiet and alert them.

Luke grunted, and Abby realized she'd been leaning extra hard on him for support. "I'm sorry," she muttered.

"No, it's all right," he said. "But I've been thinking—if Kaliman is dead set on sacrificing the goat, what are we going to do when we get there?"

Abby bit her lip. "I don't know. God can give us an idea if we pray."

Luke gazed at her. "I'll pray," he vowed. Abby could see his eyes were full of trust in God's goodness.

You're getting good at that, she thought.

Paloa had pushed ahead of them, energized by her need to rescue her pet.

Luke abruptly put an end to Abby's thoughts when he pulled them both up short. The smell of sulphur assaulted Abby's nose. Ahead of them, they could see Paloa on the edge of the clearing, one hand pressed over her mouth as she took in the scene before her.

A group of seven island men stood near the table rock. On the white rock tiny Timor was pressed down by many hands. Kaliman stood with a long, wavy-bladed knife held aloft. Abby knew it was a *kris,* the knife some islanders believed had magical powers!

The silver blade glinted in the sunlight as Kaliman raised it high above Timor. When the frightened kid bleated, it sounded as though he cried, "Ma-a-aaa-a."

Paloa dashed into the clearing, her long black hair streaming out behind her as she screamed, "No, Father!"

Chapter Nineteen

Kaliman's hand wavered as he glanced back to see
Paloa sprinting toward him. Even from this
distance, Abby could see amazement etched on his
features.

"He's my best friend! Don't hurt him!" Paloa
shouted as she reached the group of men. They
turned toward Kaliman in confusion. Perhaps
because she had spoken in English, he answered in
it.

"We must!" Kaliman roared.

Luke and Abby were hurrying toward Paloa when
a giant tremor jolted them and sent them sprawling.

Abby heard rocks splitting and crashing around
them. The mountain high above them seemed to be
coming apart!

Luke jumped up and propelled Abby firmly to a
stand. As they ran to get Paloa, they saw her use the
confusion to grab Timor from the sacrificial stone.
She hugged him to her chest, then set him on the
ground and grabbed the leash still attached to his
collar.

Kaliman and the other men stared upward, and Abby's gaze followed theirs. She gasped. The volcano belched clouds of smoke and fire. Lani was right! *Bakat's volcano is erupting, and we're standing at its feet.*

Horrified, Abby gripped Paloa's arm. "We have to go!" And yet she knew she could never outrun a volcano!

Then Kaliman put out a muscular arm to stop his daughter. "Wait. This sacrifice is needed!" He stared fiercely at her.

But the earth turned to waves, tossing everyone like boats on a choppy sea. Rocks hit the ground around them—huge chunks of hot rocks from the interior of the earth.

"Volcano!" Luke shouted, grabbing Abby's hand. "There's no time to lose. We've got to get out of here."

"We can't leave Paloa." Abby stepped toward her friend. She saw Kaliman holding out a hand toward Timor. "Give me the goat," he said.

Paloa shook her head and took a step backward. She bumped into Abby, who steadied her. "We've got to go, Paloa!" Already steam hissed and ash spewed heavenward. The cascade of hot debris increased.

"Run!" Luke yelled, yanking Abby with him. Abby grabbed for Paloa's hand, and the three of them began to fly down the incline, trying to outrun the rain of the burning death. For one brief

second Abby thought, *Oh, the poor butterflies!* Then
back into the forest they sped, with Timor galloping
behind on his leash, bleating in fear.

The men were right behind them when a thun-
derous noise rumbled like a freight train crashing
down a mountainside. Luke looked back wide-eyed.
Abby turned to see a dirty gray cloud thundering
toward them. They'd never outrun the gaseous fire
and hail. "The cave!" Abby yelled over the din,
hoping Luke heard. He veered off the path toward
the cave they'd discovered days before.

Trees crashed behind them as the powerful wave
of burning debris sped down the mountainside like
an avalanche. The whole world seemed to be
exploding, crashing, and sizzling like a giant slab of
bacon on a cosmic skillet.

Fear spurred them on quickly to the cave mouth.
The tiny mud volcanoes were now twice their original height, belching gallons of goo.

Smoke and ash began to envelop them as Luke
leapt into the narrow hollow of the cave entrance. He
turned and half-lifted Abby down. There was no time
to worry about scorpions now, no time to worry
about where this natural tunnel went. It was this or
certain death from the volcano's speeding inferno.

Luke bent down and retrieved the torch he'd

dropped five days ago, then yanked Abby deeper into the cave. Right behind them were Paloa and Kaliman, with the others on their heels. Abby coughed on the choking haze that descended over the cave entrance and began to fill it. But Luke didn't pause. He hauled her forward into the dark, tripping and scraping against stones in the blackness so the others could get in out of the thundering ash bank.

One hundred feet in, Luke stopped and grabbed Abby's hand, thrusting the unlit torch in it. It was black as ink. "Hold it," he said. "I brought my Chinese matches." It took a full minute to get one to flare, but finally the torch took. The men behind them murmured. Even though they spoke in a foreign tongue, Abby could hear the relief in their voices at the light Luke had provided.

Luke held the torch aloft and led everyone on. In the closed, stuffy cave Abby felt as though she couldn't get enough air in her lungs. The ash and gases seemed to be following them down the rock corridor.

"Hurry," Luke urged as he held the torch in front of him. Abby stayed right behind him, keeping her eyes either on the tunnel floor, so she wouldn't trip, or on Luke's back and the rope coil that bounced over his shoulder. When she wondered how the men behind her could see and paused to look, Paloa bumped into her. Kaliman snorted as one of the men crashed into his back. They were clustered in a tight knot, Abby saw, which is how they were able to see the flame and keep up the pace.

Abby spurted forward to catch up with Luke. Because of the danger, her adrenaline was pumping and she had extra energy. But as they went deeper and deeper into the unknown fissure, Abby grew exhausted. The cave eventually widened, but it also tightened from top to bottom. Luke and the other men now had to bend over slightly to keep from bumping their heads.

Suddenly Luke threw back his left arm, smacking Abby in the stomach.

"Umph! Luke, next time give me a warning."

"I didn't have one, Abby!"

She peered around his arm and gasped. A huge cavern opened up before them—and Luke was now able to stand up straight. But as he held the torch higher, Abby realized why he'd come to a crashing halt. They were close to the rim of a wide basin that was full of bubbling, burning-hot mud. It gulped and gurgled in gaseous bubbles that stunk of rotten eggs.

"Yuck, sulphur," Luke said.

The thick brown mud splattered everywhere, coating the floor near their feet and the rock walls.

"Oh no!" Abby cried out. "How are we going to get by this?"

Chapter Twenty

Kaliman pushed through his men and joined them near the edge of the mud lake. He said something that sounded to Abby like an Indonesian curse as he paced furiously.

The men behind them began talking all at once, and Paloa translated. "They say this is all my fault. I stopped the sacrifice, and now death will claim us."

Anger, like lava, boiled up in Abby. "No!" she shouted, turning to Kaliman. "Stop blaming Paloa for a volcano! Everything is under God's control—not that stupid mountain's."

Kaliman stopped pacing and his eyes narrowed in anger. "You," he said, pointing a long finger at her, "displease gods and have no respect."

Abby breathed in and counted to five. "I'm sorry. I shouldn't have yelled . . . and I didn't mean to be disrespectful, but God *is* here—the One True God—and if we pray to Him, He will help us, not kill us."

For a moment Kaliman's features softened, almost as if he appreciated her words. He began pacing silently again, and his men backed out of his way. Abby, meanwhile, bit her lip.

She heard Luke groan. "What are we going to do? Fire behind us, burning mud in front of us . . ." He sat down on a mud-spattered boulder and put his head in his left hand. The torch dipped toward the ground, and Abby rescued it from his limp grasp.

She lifted the torch and stepped cautiously around the edge of the churning lake. It appeared to meet the cavern walls on each side. "If only we had a boat," she mumbled.

Kaliman came toward her. "Even with boat, it could have acid in mud that eat through wood . . . or human skin."

"Oh, dear," she said. As she glanced at Paloa, she saw that her friend's dark eyes were full of fear. Abby wanted to comfort her. "Don't worry. God has a plan to help us."

Lord, Abby prayed silently, *please help us!* She gazed about the 40-foot wide cavern. Could they squeeze by on an edge? To her left, a stone ledge did extend out several inches over the bubbling mud. But it looked slick. She couldn't be sure in the wavering light if it continued around the bubbling lake. Abby approached it.

Yes, here was a ledge they might be able to navigate. She lifted the torch higher. *Oh, Lord, let it work!* Abby stepped out on it. The ledge was splattered with slick goo. If she should slip, she would fall into the roiling lake. Would she die instantly?

Though dangerous, she just had to know if the ledge continued around the lake.

Abby held the torch in her right hand and took several more steps with her back pressed against the cavern wall. The outcropping on which she balanced was only 10 or 12 inches wide. But it was enough—barely.

Slowly she inched around. The talking had stopped. Abby glanced back to the shore. Every eye was trained on her. Luke leapt up and came toward her. "You want me to take the torch?" he asked as he stepped onto the ledge and came toward her.

"Yes," she whispered. Slowly she handed him the firebrand and paused to rest. Then she inched on. Paloa was the next to join them. She dragged Timor with her, though he bleated his disapproval. But as a goat, he manuevered more safely than the rest. And that's what gave Abby the idea.

"Paloa," she said, "let's let Timor blaze our trail!"

Luke held out the flare and grinned. "He'll do it, I bet. Goats are uncanny at climbing in tight places."

Paloa's eyes lit up. "Yes, but you'll need to back up so he can go first."

Abby and Luke quickly agreed and retraced their steps. Paloa tied the leash onto his collar so it wouldn't drag. Then she urged the small goat out onto the ledge. The tiny kid had gotten used to the idea, apparently, for he struck out quickly, and Paloa followed bravely behind him. Abby followed her, Luke next, Kaliman, grunting his reluctant agreement, went fourth, and the rest of the men behind him.

By the end of 15 agonizing minutes, they'd reached the halfway point. They were now in the middle of the lake, smack up against the cavern wall on an impossibly narrow ledge.

"It has come to an end," Paloa announced.

"What's come to an end?" Luke asked.

"The ledge."

Abby could hear the goat bleating in distress. She felt like bleating, too. Her legs were beginning to tremble, a sure sign that they were fatigued. *Please don't let them give out on me now,* she prayed. If they did, she'd plunge to a boiling, suffocating death. *Please help us!*

Suddenly Timor's cries sounded different. He was moving! "Where's he going?" Abby asked.

"He's found a way up!" Paloa said in amazement. "He's climbing higher."

"He's taking the high way," Abby said with a grin. She peered as best she could around Paloa. The goat stood gazing down on Paloa, bleating an encouragement for her to follow.

"Can you get up there?" Luke asked. "I can't stand here much longer—I'm starting to slip."

Paloa carefully placed one hand on the higher rock ledge and twisted her body to face it. The toes of her sandals were all that balanced on the rock ledge as she cautiously lifted one foot to put on a higher stone. Slowly she pulled herself up to the higher ledge. "Come on, Abby. Timor is eager to press on."

Abby followed her friend's lead, heart pounding, hands moist with perspiration. She hated ledges, heights, and the possibility of falling. *God, help me.* As she, too, balanced on her toes, she lifted her right leg and bumped it into a stone outcropping. Instantly she lost her balance and began to slip. Grasping with her hands, she clung.

She could hear Luke's indrawn breath and now felt his wide hand splayed on her back. "That's a girl," he said, "nice and easy. Lift yourself up, you're almost there. . . ."

Abby pulled. Her muscles strained, but she made it. Luke followed quickly as she went forward on hands and knees behind Paloa and Timor.

That stone ledge lasted for 25 feet and then dropped away onto a tumble of wide boulders that were easy to climb down. The goat jumped lightly from stone to stone and waited for them at the muddy bottom. Luke helped Abby clamber down, carrying the torch and lighting the way.

"Thank God," he whispered to her, "the tunnel continues. If it hadn't, we'd truly be trapped. Who knows, but the cave entrance might be blocked with rocks and trees by now." He led them down the stone fissure. It was narrow, and they had to go single file.

They'd only gone on a few minutes when a distant rumble tore through the heart of the earth.

Abby's pulse raced in fear. Was the earth going to explode under their feet or bury them alive? The last man in line screamed something in his language.

Luke stopped to hear Paloa's shouts. "Something's coming down the cave toward us!" she screamed.

Men crowded forward, tearing past Abby, pushing and shoving. In the pandemonium, one grabbed the torch from Luke and sped on. And then Abby and Luke, now last in line, heard it, too. The sound of rushing water, perhaps.

"Mud," Luke said, pushing Abby ahead of him.

The cave entrance had not been blocked! Abby instantly knew a *lahar* was upon them.

Chapter Twenty-One

"There must be a giant mud slide coming down the mountain," Luke panted as he urged Abby to go faster. "Either it's pouring into the cave—or maybe it's the mud lake exploding. Hurry!"

The terrifying noise swelled in volume, and Abby pushed herself with all her might, but the man with the torch was way ahead of them now. When she tripped, Luke plucked her up and grabbed her arm. As the tunnel widened, he moved beside her. The thundering noise grew louder, and it sucked the courage from Abby's heart. The cave trembled under the coming onslaught.

Just as Abby feared they would be overwhelmed, they saw light ahead. Within seconds they broke into the open daylight, except that smoke and ash had darkened the sky. Small pebbles were still raining down all around them.

"The secret grotto!" Abby cried, hurrying toward Paloa and Kaliman who were just exiting the shallow cave with a bundle under Kaliman's arm. Timor bleated and strained on his leash to get away.

There was no time to lose! Abby and Luke dashed after Paloa and her father as they raced into the beach tunnel.

As soon as they jogged into the darkness, they saw a flickering light ahead. Kaliman's men with the torch were waiting for them to catch up! Now the flame bobbed and danced just 15 feet ahead of them, and Abby and Luke were able to follow.

But within seconds of sprinting into the cave, a giant wave of mud shot out of the volcanic tunnel they'd just left and exploded into the secret grotto. Half its force was diffused as it flooded everywhere, but a great quantity of the mudflow poured into the beach tunnel. Abby, last in line, was struck by a thick wave of warm mud that hit her legs. She crashed against Luke.

Seconds later, they both lay in a stinking pool of mud and debris. The wind had been knocked from them, and Abby took a long moment to open her eyes. When she did, Paloa's sweet face hung over her, concern evident. "Are you okay?" Paloa asked gently, placing a palm on Abby's cheek.

Abby nodded and slowly sat up. "But I can't seem to stay clean. . . . Luke!"

Luke was lying facedown in a mud puddle. Abby turned him over and wiped off the goo from his eyes and lips with the hem of her scarf. "Luke! Are you all right?"

She laid her head on his chest to listen for breathing, for a heartbeat, for anything. . . .

Then she heard his stomach grumble loudly with hunger. He couldn't be dead! Abby straightened and gazed at his face, which was now covered in a ridiculous grin.

"You varmint! You scared me to death!"

Laughter rang out as the men gathered around and offered hands to help them both up. Kaliman's stern features softened as he nodded. "Good, you are safe. Let us move on. I must hurry to check on village."

Instantly the men headed out, the atmosphere sober again as each person probably thought of loved ones at home. How had the village fared— and Abby's family?

Ten minutes later Abby saw the cave exit within reach. They'd made it! They'd survived the volcano, the mud lake, the *lahar*. With the cave opening above the beach, Abby knew they'd be home with Ma and Pa in half an hour. All they had to do was hurry down the long curving beach to the mansion.

But as Abby left the tunnel's darkness and walked into the gray light of day, she saw the men bunched in a tight knot just outside the cave. Their voices were quiet but urgent.

"Look," Luke said, pointing. Abby saw his green eyes narrow. She quickly followed his gaze and gasped.

About 20 yards below the cave four giant dragons swept the sandy path with their long powerful tails. Their bright yellow tongues flicked in and out, scenting the ash-laden wind. Their heads swung back and forth in agitation. *They're stirred up by the disaster,* Abby realized. "Oh, Luke," she said, "what are we going to do? We can't go up from here."

But her thoughts were interrupted by Kaliman, who stalked back toward her angrily. "Do you see what comes of not sacrificing goat?" His finger stabbed the air in front of her face. "The volcano god called on dragons to kill us—to eat us!"

Abby was shocked when tenderhearted Paloa came to her side and bravely took her hand. "This is not Abby's fault, Father," Paloa said softly. "It is just the earth erupting because it was time to erupt, and those are just hungry beasts. God got us through the tunnel and around that lake of burning mud. So I am very sure that if we pray, He will help us now, too."

A heavy sigh, like steam, gushed from Kaliman. In frustration he threw Paloa's cloth-wrapped bundle onto the dirt.

"No, Father," she cried as she bent to retrieve it. "This is precious." The old cloth fell off one corner, revealing part of the hidden treasure. Abby could now see that it was a small painting of a woman.

Kaliman saw it, too. Immediately he fell to his knees and plucked at the cloth to uncover the whole painting. A hush fell over the scene as he reverently picked it up. "Malaya," he said tenderly, his eyes riveted, as if he were alone with the portrait.

Abby recognized the other person in the paint-

172

ing. It was a much-younger Kaliman, standing beside his beloved wife.

Kaliman finally raised bright eyes to Paloa. "How did you get this?"

"I took it off the wall," she said with a small shrug. "A long time ago Grandmother told me I could have anything of hers, and that portrait of you and mother is all I ever wanted. I've kept it at my secret grotto for two years now. . . ." Looking worried that she'd done something wrong, she continued. "That way I could see Mother's picture any time I want. And I like seeing your face so happy, Father."

Kaliman pressed his lips together as he still knelt beside the portrait. Abby could see he was struggling not to cry. "Is my face not happy now?"

Paloa bit her lower lip. "It is often angry, Father. Forgive me." She bowed her head, her curtain of silky hair falling forward.

Kaliman swallowed hard, then rose up with the painting safely tucked under his arm. "No." He put a finger under Paloa's chin to lift her up. "Forgive me, Daughter. I am ashamed—I have blamed my own mother for something . . ."

The wind blew ash across the path. Even the scent of the sea was blotted out by the acrid breeze. Abby watched wordlessly as gray ash floated onto Paloa's dark hair. She suddenly understood why Paloa had never shared the picture with them. It showed Kaliman the way he used to be, the way she wished he could be now.

Kaliman shook his head hopelessly. "Let us get back, there is much to . . ." But when he glanced up, he must have remembered the giant lizards blocking their path. The men behind him shifted uneasily again. "We are doomed. . . ." Kaliman plopped down on a boulder and put his head in his hands. "I should have sacrificed goat. Now, is too late."

Luke snorted in disagreement. "The reason those beasts are here is because of the volcano!"

Something about Kaliman's hopelessness got to Abby. There was such fear in his brown eyes. "It doesn't matter why those dragons are here," she said kindly. "What matters is that God is here, too."

Abby watched the dragons' thick bodies stalk the area. *Living dinosaurs,* Uncle Samuel had said. *Stealth predators,* Mrs. Cleets had written. She thought of walking past them and her skin prickled with anxiety. *They are the scariest beasts I've ever seen . . . so powerful and quick, Lord. Our flesh could be ripped apart in seconds . . . and I'm so slow! But Pa said that there's always a way of escape.*

What had Pa said? "God has a way to deliver you—it's called the Trust-in-Him Highway!"

Abby closed her eyes and lifted her heart to God.

A soft breeze blew across Abby as she prayed out loud, "Dear Lord, please help us find a way of escape."

DO NOT FEAR, FOR I AM WITH YOU . . . I WILL

UPHOLD YOU WITH MY RIGHTEOUS RIGHT HAND.

But, Lord, we need a good idea—an idea like Stuart had to outwit his dragon.

DO NOT BE AFRAID OF THE TERROR BY DAY, FOR I WILL GIVE MY ANGELS CHARGE CONCERNING YOU— TO GUARD YOU IN ALL YOUR WAYS.

Tears pooled beneath Abby's closed eyes as faith swelled like puffed-up rice, pushing out the fear.

Thank You, Jesus.

When she opened her eyes, her gaze landed on Luke. The coiled, mud-caked rope, still wrapped around his chest, drew her attention. Abby glanced toward the distant safety of the shore. The dragons were directly below them, on the sloping path. But there were trees dotting the area.

One tree in particular stood beyond the dragons. "Perhaps," she said, "perhaps it's just close enough. . . ."

Chapter Twenty-Two

Luke cocked his head at Abby. "What's close enough?"

"That tree," she said, pointing. "If we could throw your rope so it catches in the branches, we could go *over* the dragons."

Luke nodded. "A great idea, *Pelanduk!*" He began scouting the ground immediately. "We'll need something to tie on the end so when we toss it, it'll catch between some branches."

Kaliman, listening, also began searching the area. Everyone scattered to look for something they might be able to use, but it was Kaliman who whistled to call them all back. He held up a fairly stout piece of driftwood. Silverish and weathered, it was about three feet long and perhaps five inches in diameter.

Luke took the rope off and quickly tied a reef knot in the middle of the branch. "Do you think it'll reach?" Abby asked.

"We'll soon know!" Luke said as he hefted the

silvery driftwood in his right hand. He weighed it carefully and closed his eyes briefly.

Is he praying? Abby wondered.

For a split second Abby thought of David and Goliath. Then the wood left Luke's hand and flew like a spear through the smoky air. "The battle is the Lord's!" Abby whispered.

When it crashed into the green-leafed tree some 20 yards away, Abby held her breath. It disappeared. But would it hold when they jerked on it?

Kaliman had a grip on the end of the rope, and he hadn't much left. But he began to tug on it. About a yard or two of rope coiled in, but it finally jerked to a halt. He pulled several times.

It held! The men pounded on each other's backs in jubilation.

Abby hugged Luke around the neck. "Good job!" she gushed.

He dimpled. "Proves that God was guiding it," he said quietly.

Everyone was smiling but Paloa, who burst into tears. "What is it?" Abby asked.

"It's Timor!" she wailed. "What will I do with Timor?"

Suddenly Abby realized she didn't know. "Oh, Luke," she said, turning desperate eyes on him. "Timor can't go hand over hand—and neither can I!" She'd never had a strong grip. And she'd never been able to do hand over hands on tree limbs for more than a few feet without losing her grip and falling. "I can't go all that way on a rope that's 25 feet above the ground!" She felt like crying now, too.

Luke swallowed hard. "I'll carry you, Abby."

"No, Luke, it's too much for you. . . . We wouldn't make it." She turned away and stared at the rope, their way of escape! But not for her.

When she felt a warm hand on her shoulder, Abby turned back and was surprised to see Kaliman's dark eyes staring into hers. "I know of a way," he said gruffly. He reached down and untied Abby's *batik* silk scarf and held it up. The ocean breeze whipped it upward. Then Kaliman pointed at Luke's knotted rope belt that looped through his sailor pants. "Abby will wear that belt," Kaliman said, "and we tie this to belt. It will go over that rope," he said, pointing to the rope that spanned the distance.

Luke broke into a cautious smile. "I think it'll work, Abby." He unknotted his belt and tied it securely around her waist. Then Kaliman knotted one end of the long scarf onto the belt on one of Abby's sides. He walked her down the incline a short way, then tossed the other end of the scarf over the rope and tied it to the other side of her belt.

Abby's head would just miss the rope as she hung from the scarf and, hopefully, sailed down the rope slide to the tree.

Kaliman gauged the distance from the cliffside to

the tree. "I go first so someone be there to catch you. You—ah—might go pretty fast. . . ."

Abby's stomach clenched at the thought of dangling up so high.

"What about Timor?" Paloa said, her face tense with worry.

"I'll stuff him in my shirt," Luke volunteered. "Will he stay quiet and not kick me?"

Paloa grinned at him gratefully. "Oh yes!" She bent down to give Timor a lecture. "You be still and let Luke carry you!"

She picked up the tiny kid and cuddled him, then stuffed him in the shirt Luke had just unbuttoned. Luke grimaced as he rebuttoned his shirt and tucked it in. "I sure hope it holds," he said.

Paloa tucked the prized portrait under her waist-band in the back.

"Paloa," Kaliman said, "climb on." He bent down and motioned for her to wrap her arms around his neck. "I will carry you across."

"Oh, Father!" She did as he'd commanded and looked back at Abby and Luke with a smile. Muscular Kaliman gripped the rope and began going hand over hand, hanging 10, 15, then 25 feet above the ground as the cliff fell away. Abby watched nervously as they got halfway across, then two-thirds. A few minutes later they arrived at the tree and Paloa was waving from among the green leaves.

Minutes passed as two more men started on their journey through the air. No more than two at a

time, Kaliman had ordered, so the rope would not
be too stressed. The goat became impatient, and
Luke finally took him out and set him down. He
put a foot on Timor's leash so he wouldn't get away.

Finally the last man climbed into the tree
branches. All but Kaliman had left the tree and
headed toward the water. They were eager, Abby
knew, to check on their own families in the village.

"Your turn," Luke said, smiling encouragement.

Abby took a deep breath. "You think it will
hold?"

"Yep, I do. Silk is incredibly strong—we learned
that in China, remember? God won't let you down,
Abby." She nodded, but her stomach was doing
flips.

"Okay, I'm gonna give you a little push to get you
started. The rest of the way is downhill, so you
should fly right into Kaliman's arms."

With that Luke pushed her back while Abby
stepped forward off the cliff edge. She instantly
soared out over the sloping ground and whizzed
over the path. Grabbing each side of the scarf, she
hung on for dear life. In a gray blur she saw the
dirt-caked dragons below her. They smelled her
scent and moved around, growling and hissing at
each other. But in mere seconds she flew over them
and on another 30 feet to the tree, where Kaliman
had placed himself to break her landing. She
laughed as she thudded into him and he quickly
untied her and lifted her up to sit near Paloa.

Now they turned to see Luke's progress. But he wasn't dangling on the rope! He was chasing Timor about on the rocks as the little goat tried to escape his clutches.

"No, no, no!" Paloa said. "You naughty kid!"

Abby's eyes widened in fear. All the commotion and Timor's bleating were drawing the dragons' attention. Two had started up the incline! Luke had to leave at once!

"Luke, the dragons are coming!" Abby exclaimed.

One dragon streaked quickly toward Timor, who was still six feet from Luke.

"Oh, Lord!" Abby cried. "Help Luke!" Her fingers dug into the tree branch.

Luke lunged toward Timor, caught him by one leg, and dragged the reluctant kid to him. He'd rebuttoned most of his shirt, so he now stuffed the overexcited creature inside again and leapt toward the rope. Seconds later the first dragon reached the very spot Luke had been standing and lunged toward the rope. The rope shook and trembled as the beast landed on it, then backed off. Luke now dangled in the air 10 feet away. Abby saw the fear on his face, the white-knuckled grip he had on the rope. *Why isn't he going hand over hand?* she wondered. *Why is he just hanging there?*

Then she saw it. Timor was kicking and moving inside his shirt! If the goat didn't quit, Luke's shirt would rip, and Timor could fall to his death. She glanced toward Paloa, whose eyes were closed and whose lips were moving in silent prayer.

When Abby peered back to Luke, he was moving again and the goat had quieted in his shirt.

Soon Luke reached the tree, though sweat streamed from his face and neck. "Whew!" he sighed in relief. "That was tough, no *kidding!*"

Perhaps because everything had been tense for so long, Abby burst into laughter.

"Shhh!" Luke said. "You want the dragons to come looking for us?"

She bit her lip and quickly followed his lead as he pointed to the spots where she should step to get safely down the tree. Once on the ground they hurried toward the water's edge and followed the long curving beach toward the mansion.

Chapter Twenty-Three

Abby could see people milling about on the shore and only one ship at anchor in the small blue bay.

When a woman with brown hair left the group and ran toward Abby, she knew it was her mother. Abby's legs were so weary, but she willed herself to hurry forward. The look on Ma's face was one of intense relief. Tears leaked from the corners of her eyes. "Thank God!" she cried. "You're safe." Ma reached out to embrace Luke, too.

"Your pa wouldn't let us go into the forest when we discovered you were missing," Ma continued. "The volcano's huge ash bank came very close to the mansion. It was too dangerous." Overcome with emotion, Charlotte Kendall simply pulled Abby close and held on.

When Abby looked up she saw that Sarah had grabbed on to her skirt and was hugging her around the waist. Abby patted her back.

"I was so worried about you," Sarah said, "that I got a really bad tummy ache."

"Thanks, Sarah," Abby said, smiling. "I couldn't ask for a better sister."

While Luke hugged Sarah, too, Pa and Duncan, Uncle Samuel and Lani all gathered round to make sure Abby and Luke were safe. Abby heard Luke explaining to Uncle Samuel how they'd escaped the eruption by going underground. "That was brilliant," she heard Uncle Samuel exclaim.

As things began to settle down, Abby saw that Sulia was holding Paloa close and Kaliman was standing off a ways watching them. Then he squared his shoulders, as if a decision had been made, and started through the sand toward them.

Sulia was smoothing Paloa's long hair off her shoulder when Kaliman touched her on the back. She turned, and her face blanched.

"Mother," he started out. For a minute he seemed too choked up to speak, so he simply held out the painting. Sulia's eyes widened in surprise.

"I accused you of keeping this from me," he said. "But I was wrong. Can you forgive me?"

Sulia's face softened. "Of course, Kaliman. I will love you forever—and I thank you for your apology."

He went straight into her arms, his muscled frame somehow fitting into the embrace of the tiny, aging woman. Paloa surged forward to wrap her small arms around them both. Together they stood and hugged, a family once again. Abby's heart caught at the sight of Paloa's radiant face. A lump formed in her throat as she thought, *God truly does order our steps. . . . Now I see why He led us here—to an island with deadly dragons and erupting volcanoes! It was to help Paloa, Sulia, and Kaliman.*

"But how did you find the painting?" Sulia asked when they separated.

"*I* took it, Grandmother," Paloa admitted. "I didn't know Father was looking for it, and you had said to take anything I wanted. . . ."

"Of course," Sulia said, nodding. "I should have guessed."

Before any more could be discussed, Kaliman's men returned from their hike up the beach. They quickly learned that the volcano's destructive flow had cut a path between the mansion and the village, which was two miles away. They couldn't reach it at this time, at least not on foot, because of a *lahar* that had run in that direction, too.

As the men milled about, worried, Pa offered to sail them around the point to check on their families. But no sooner had they agreed when three small sailboats skimmed over the bay waters and dropped anchor close to shore. Kaliman waved, and Sulia smiled as she stood in the surf waiting to greet people.

Paloa came toward Abby and Luke. "Those are people from my village. We will soon learn how it has fared."

The first people ashore spoke rapidly in their Indonesian dialect. Paloa translated for Abby. "He says that the village is mostly destroyed by the volcano! All the people ran to their boats and are on their way here."

Instantly Abby saw that more sails dotted the bay. The whole village was arriving, carrying whatever they could in their escape: pigs, goats, squawking chickens. Soon the shoreline was littered with families and children, animals and belongings. Mothers who'd lost track of their little ones were reunited onshore. Neighbors had grabbed children and tossed them into their own little ships and sailed them to safety.

"Oh, how wonderful," Abby said, her eyes moist as she watched a mother kneel and grab hold of her lost child, hugging through sobs.

"Of course," Paloa said sweetly, "it is the Indonesian way, *tolong menolong*—neighbors helping neighbors."

Abby saw Sulia speaking in her native tongue to the people onshore and directing them to follow her to the mansion. "What is your grandmother saying?" she asked.

Paloa grinned. "She is saying, 'Come to my home to refresh yourselves. My home is your home for as long as you want. I am so happy to have you here!' "

Ma joined them and sighed contentedly. "All's well that ends well. I don't think Sulia will ever be lonely again."

When Kaliman stepped toward them, Luke and

Ma opened the circle to include him. "My mother will not live alone again," he said, nodding at Charlotte.

Then he pierced Abby with his dark gaze. "You have opened my eyes. I see that my mother's God *does* answer prayer. We came home safely even if we did not sacrifice little goat. So I will welcome her Bible reading from now on. And," he paused as if the rest were hard to say, "and I thank you for helping us."

Warmth flooded Abby. "I'm glad we could do a little," she said, "but it was only *tolong menolong*—neighbors helping neighbors—the way Jesus said we should."

Kaliman threw back his head and laughed. "You learn quick, Abby Kendall. Maybe I can do the same."

Two days later, Abby's ship was ready to set sail. They had new barrels of water, extra provisions of fruit, and a wonderful adventure to remember. Twenty-two men from Kaliman's village had set off, the day after the volcano, with the nets and ropes from the old warehouse and had captured the four and only remaining giant dragons lurking two miles away.

Once they were immobilized in the nets, the men had wrapped their ferocious jaws shut with rope so they couldn't bite anyone. Then Duncan and their crew had sailed the *Kamana* down the beach and taken the beasts aboard. Not actually aboard, but using pullies, they'd hung them over the sides. One off the port bow and one off the starboard bow. Another hung from the port stern and the last one from the starboard stern. At first the beasts had tried to thrash free, but they'd finally given up and grown quiet.

It was only fitting, Abby thought, that they do this neighborly thing for their new friends. And it had been Sarah's idea—for she didn't want Timor or Paloa to be endangered again. Duncan promised to deliver the beasts to the land from which they'd been taken: Komodo Island, in the southern seas. The very area marked, *Here Be Dragons*!

Pa and Uncle Samuel wound in the anchor chain and went aloft to unfurl the sails. The sun's first golden-pink rays broke over the horizon like spilled honey. A gentle wind snapped the canvas. Abby listened happily to the familiar sounds of the rigging and timbers creaking.

"We'll sail south," Duncan said as he twirled his dark moustache, "and drop off the cargo at Komodo Island, as Sarah suggested."

Abby glanced over at the incredibly fierce baggage hanging off the four points of the ship.

She was fascinated by them—now that they were safely bound. Abby joined Sarah and Uncle Samuel at the stern, where he leaned over the side and examined the dragon's dirt-encrusted scales. Although its dinosaur head could not bite them, its long yellow tongue snaked up through the net toward them.

Sarah stepped back. "Yuck, that tongue stinks!" she exclaimed. "He needs to brush his teeth."

Uncle Samuel chuckled. "I think that bad breath is how the tales began about fire-breathing dragons."

Lani was sitting on the railing nearest the dragon when its long yellow tongue shot out again and missed her wrist by an inch. Uncle Samuel reacted with lightning speed, yanking her into his arms and away from the dangerous beast.

The fear on his face seemed to touch her. Abby watched in surprise as Lani laid a palm against Uncle Samuel's pork-chop sideburn. "You are so wonderful to me," she said tenderly. For a moment, Uncle Samuel stood still, then he bent over and kissed the beautiful half-Hawaiian woman. Abby's eyes widened in surprise as she kissed him back!

Sarah moaned. "Yuck!"

But Abby turned to Luke. "It burst into flames," she said, "just like I knew it would!"

"What are you talking about?" he asked, apparently confused.

"Shhh!" she said, waving her hand to silence him. But she didn't need to because Luke, too, was mesmerized by the scene unfolding before them. Oblivious to the others, Uncle Samuel kneeled on the slanting deck and cradled Lani's hand. He looked up at her with shining eyes and solemnly said, "Lani, I love you. Will you marry me?"

For a second nothing moved but Lani's long chestnut hair blowing in the breeze. She pursed her lips to keep from crying, then burst out, "Yes! Yes, Samuel! I will!"

Uncle Samuel shot up and picked her up off the deck and swung her around. Suddenly everyone surrounded them, laughing and clapping the engaged couple on the back. Abby caught sight of Duncan wiping away tears with the back of his hand; then he pumped Samuel's hand in a congratulatory shake.

"Welcome to the family! 'Tis a bonnie lass ye've got, man. Take good carrre of herrr."

Ma and Lani embraced and cried, then laughed and cried some more. "Oh, we have to start planning for the wedding right away," Ma said.

"Why not just let 'em get hitched tonight?" Pa suggested. "Duncan, as sea captain, can perform the ceremony."

Lani looked horror-stricken. "I've always dreamed of having a wedding with plumeria in my hair."

"Plumerias?" Uncle Samuel asked.

"Oh, Samuel," Lani said, her turquoise eyes brimming with eager joy, "can we please stop in

Tahiti on the way home to get married? It would be something to remember for the rest of our lives! I've always wanted to go to the homeland of my people—to paradise!"

"Tahiti, plumerias, whatever you want, Lani." Uncle Samuel, the absentminded biologist, had just become Uncle Samuel, the absentminded groom. It was bound to get worse, Abby thought, before the wedding actually took place.

"Tahiti!" Luke whooped. "Another port to add to our list."

But before Abby could think any more on the wedding, she heard Paloa's voice ringing over the bay waters. *"Aloha, Abby!"*

Abby grinned, for she had taught Paloa that Hawaiian word. *"Aloha!"* Abby yelled back as she waved wildly. It was a perfect word to say good-bye, because it also meant "hello" and "I love you." There was hope in *aloha*, Abby thought, just as there was hope in Paloa's life now.

The sun was beginning to set and the sky had turned pink and gray when they sighted the dry barren hills of Komodo. Luke got the privilege of yanking the first rope and dropping the biggest dragon into the dark blue sea.

The water offshore was rough, but the lizard's

giant tail instantly began to thrash the sea, shrugging off the net, and churning the blue to froth as it beat its way toward the sloping sandy beach.

As the others were released, they, too, lashed their tails back and forth, swimming easily in the waves. They followed the first one toward the sandy point.

Luke joined Abby, watching the powerful creatures disappear as their dark scales merged against the dark blue water. Then they were gone. Abby realized she might never see another dragon as long as she lived. That would definitely be all right with her!

The wind had picked up, and she shivered a bit. "Luke," she said, "it's a little scary knowing there are so many dangerous beasts in the world. So many dangers everywhere we go . . . I mean, even the Bible says that the serpent fell from heaven and landed on earth. . . ."

Luke nodded. "But listen to this, Abby." He retrieved his Bible from a day pack he'd set on a bulkhead. "I was just reading an hour ago." He opened his Bible and flipped through the New Testament, stopping at John 17. "This is a prayer Jesus prayed to His heavenly Father before He faced our greatest enemy—death—and just before He overcame death and rose again:

'My prayer is not that You take them out of the world but that You protect them from the evil one.' "

Abby gazed at Luke and saw peace shining from his eyes.

"Jesus was talking about us," he said. "We're here in a dangerous world, but God's here, too, just like you told Kaliman. That means no matter what serpents we face here on earth, the Spirit of the Lord is here to keep us safe. . . . He'll never leave us or forsake us, Abigail Kendall. And with His help, I won't ever let you down either."

For a moment, Abby was touched by Luke's loving-kindness. Then she watched his face pucker into a mischievous grin.

"And frankly, Abigail, you need someone like me, a valiant knight in shining armor. Yep, Sir Quiggley of the Round Table sounds pretty good. Because if there ever was a damsel who got into more distress than you, I haven't met her yet."

"Luke Quiggley, the only table you're familiar with is the dinner table!"

"You're charming when those blue eyes narrow," Luke said casually, "and your nostrils flare."

"Not half as charming as Sir Quiggley in a skirt!" she shot back. When Luke's face flushed red under his freckles, Abby jumped up in alarm. She raced to the ratlines and climbed up three, six, twelve feet above the deck.

He stood below, a frown on his face.

"Now, Luke, remember—" she said sweetly, "the fruit of the Spirit is *self-control!*"

He began climbing the ratlines. Abby squealed

and headed higher, clinging anxiously to the wobbly ropes. With the ship's brisk pace, the movement was magnified at this height.

Suddenly Luke was beside her, grinning. "Had enough, Carrottop?"

Abby scowled at the familiar nickname.

"Remember," Luke admonished, "the fruit of the Spirit is also *patience,* which makes a good middle name for people who need reminding."

He was referring, of course, to *her* middle name, so Abby laughed in spite of herself. "I give," she said, starting to climb down.

Luke put out a hand to stop her. "See the sunset?" He nodded at the flaming horizon. "It looks like dragon fire."

Abby gazed at the bank of fiery clouds. Gold swords arced through them, and peace settled over her along with the last pink rays. "Dragon fire? Let it come. We've got the shield of faith to see us through."

> I waited patiently for the Lord; He turned to me and heard my cry. He lifted me out of the slimy pit, out of the mud and mire; He set my feet on a rock and gave me a firm place to stand. He put a new song in my mouth, a hymn of praise to our God. Many will see and fear and put their trust in the Lord.
>
> Psalm 40:1-3

SOUTHERN MOLUCCAS

BANDA SEA

Nila

Teun

Babar

Tepa

Sermata

Damar

TUTUKEY

Moa

Romang

Gunungapi

Kisar

WETAR

TIMOR

N

Alor

FROM CHINA

Don't miss the next exciting adventure in
the South Seas Adventures series:

Abby
Trouble
in Tahiti

Sail with Abby to beautiful Tahiti, with its waving palm trees, grass huts, and glistening black-sand beach. It's the perfect spot for a wedding of a lifetime—and to learn how to black-pearl dive. But do dangers loom just below the lovely aquamarine water? And why has the queen's right-hand man imprisoned a French visitor to the island? Abby is determined to find out.

Indonesian Words

adat—to behave with manners toward others, to act becomingly as one should

babirusa—a wild pig whose tusks grow through the roof of its mouth

batik—a fabric printed by an Indonesian method of hand-printing textiles by coating with wax the parts not to be dyed

frangipani—the tree known as "plumeria" in Hawaii with sweet-smelling white and yellow or white and pink blossoms

gado-gado—a vegetable dish topped with peanut sauce

gamelan—type of drum music used for important ceremonies

kris—a wavy-bladed knife which, in folk legends, is portrayed as having magical powers

lahar—a deadly mudflow often associated with Indonesian volcanoes

musang—a catlike mammal that lives in the tops of palm trees or palm-thatched huts and eats many different insects

ora—the word used by some Indonesian islanders for Komodo dragon

pelanduk—the small 14-inch mouse deer that is beloved in Indonesian folktales for its ability to outsmart its enemies

tolong menolong—the culturally accepted idea that neighbors should always help neighbors

ular—snake

wayang—Indonesian puppet show

Nautical Words

anchor—a device usually of metal attached to a ship by a cable and cast overboard to hold the ship in a particular place

boom—a long spar used to extend the foot of a sail

bow—front of ship

brig—a two-masted, square-rigged ship

bulkhead—raised portion on deck

heel—to lean temporarily from the action of wind or waves

helm—a lever or wheel used to control the rudder of a ship for steering

mainsail—the principal sail on a mainmast

port—a harbor town where ships may take on or discharge cargo or the left side of a ship looking forward

ratline—any of the small transverse ropes attached to the shrouds of a ship so as to form the steps of a rope ladder

rigging—lines and chains used aboard a ship

starboard—the right side of a ship looking forward

stern—the back of a ship

About the Author

Like Abby, Pamela Walls once faced her own frightening adventure with giant beasts.

"While I was a student at the university in Santa Cruz, California, I did field studies on wild elephant seals during their mating and birthing season. Male seals can weigh more than a car, and they rumble along the beach like rolling water beds! These 14-foot-long beasts with long bellowing snouts go much faster than I can run on my slow legs, and they often stampede over other seals during competition for females.

"That year I saw many earthshaking battles take place as these giant males reared up and threw themselves against their opponents' necks, slashing with their teeth. Blood flew, female seals darted out of the way, and I stayed at a distance while taking notes.

"But one morning I was walking alone at the ocean's edge, taking a head count. I loved the wisps of fog blowing past me, the briny smell of the ocean. As I looked up toward the sand dunes, I counted three huge males lying on the pale-gold sand. Something startled them, and they lifted their heads and noticed me. They began to get up. For some horrible reason, other males down the beach were sitting up and taking notice, too. Since I knew a walking person looks like a threat to them, I knelt on the sand, hoping they'd ignore me. At that moment, however, two huge seals swam out of the sea and toward me through the surf! I was trapped on all sides by giant aggressive seals!

"At that instant, the earth began trembling, and I glanced back at the dunes. Those males were now charging toward me. Yikes! I couldn't outrun the steamrollers stampeding toward me! I was in mortal danger.

"But suddenly, out of the mists, a female seal on the nearby dunes got up and raced ahead of the males, straight into the waves. All the males quickly shifted their focus away from me to the fleeing female. As they barreled after her, the ground shook, and I ran down the beach. When I stopped and peered back, the female was swimming out to sea with five large males in hot pursuit. I trembled in awe as the mist blew over the prehistoric beasts that now plunged beneath the cold gray waters.

"Have you ever had a close call like that?" Pamela asks. "Maybe while you were driving, another car just barely missed yours? We sure do live in a dangerous world. Our lives can change in a nano-second. But Jesus said, 'Take heart! I have overcome the world.' (John 16:33)

"That means no matter what happens, God has already won the battle over death—and there is eternal life for us who love Him. He stands ready to help us. Through His Spirit living in us, we're equipped for any battle on earth.

"But *we* have a part to play, too; we must *have*

faith, for this pleases Him, and we must *surrender* our lives to Him. Once we do, He promises to be with us forever. Our battles become His battles—and God has never lost a fight! Nothing is too hard for Him. Sometimes He sends angels to help us. Or He can even send a female elephant seal!

"In answer to our cries, I've seen God change circumstances that hurt His children—like the time He healed my husband's cancer," Pam continues. "And I've seen Him change people's hearts (mine included)—softening them so they think more of others than themselves. Both are miracles!

"God is so wonderful, so full of love and power. You don't want to miss any of His works! So keep your eyes peeled for all the good things He's doing in your life. Praise Him and thank Him for everything, because when you do, it's like having a shield that protects you from any flaming arrows coming your way. Victory is ours because Jesus has already overcome the world. And with His help, you can, too!"

"Not by might nor by power, but by My Spirit," *says the Lord.*　　　　　　　　　　Zechariah 4:6